LOVE BETWEEN THE W(

Orlando Gomez and Mar Escribano

Mexican writer **Orlando Gomez** met Spanish writer **Mar Escribano** in September 2013. He needed to burn his soul into the paper and she wanted to escape from reality. Over the past year and a half they have collaborated on six novels and are presently writing their seventh book, which will be the first part of a trilogy. Here we present to you one of their Spanish-Mexican literary co-productions (the very first of their works together): **Love Between the words**, this is the story of Mary Smith, a 48 year old American woman, owner of the world's largest book publishing house. She is the very model of a visionary businesswoman, ethical, methodical and lucid, determined to get ahead in the world. Everything in Mary's life is order and perfection until fate lures 26 year old Andreu Santa Rosa, a Cuban baseball player of some promise to New York looking for work. The attraction between the two is so brutal that it drags us on to explore the wonders of true love, and not just the noble side that requires the ultimate sacrifice, but also the perversions that can consume and destroy.

Special thanks to all of the readers of our Spanish blog LOVE BETWEEN THE LINES, where 'someone or something' has cast a magical incantation upon us, a wonderful spell full of witchcraft and sorcery.

A big hug to all of you from us, your unconditional fans: Orlando Gomez and Mar Escribano.

© Mar Escribano and Orlando Gomez

The total or partial reproduction of this work by any means or process, either electronic or mechanical, computer processing, rental or otherwise transfer of the work without the prior written permission of the copyright holders is prohibited.

Copyright: LO 018-2014

Printed in UK - Printed in the UK

PROLOGUE

Love Between the Words is a story of love and hatred, and while it is indeed necessary to state that there are no connections between our fictional characters and real people living in the outside world, there are many Mary Smiths and many Andreus who may be our neighbors, friends or even that person that we just happened to bump into in the street when out shopping or sightseeing the other day.

Our work is dedicated to all the Mary Smiths and Andreus in the world: two antagonistic characters who represent heartbreak and love, coldness and warmth of character, mathematics as opposed to feelings. You can choose to live your life according to logical and regular rules -controlled by your brain and intellect; another human being may, however, decide to go by his heart. The choice is entirely personal, but the consequences in how we live our lives are very different, depending upon which path we choose to follow.

And thus, we now ask you our dear reader, who would you like to be? Are you going to choose Mary Smith with her behavior driven by intellect and logic or do you prefer to be Andreu, whose heart sets the rules for him to follow? That choice is entirely yours.

The two of us, Orlando Grande and Carmen Spain, present you with these two opposing paths. We do not sit in judgment; we are just the mere narrators, you and only you are the one who decides.

Our only hope is that you select the correct option, disregard the inappropriate one and that your final choice will provide you with the greatest of joys.

PART ONE: THE ORIGIN

This is the beginning of Mary Smith and Andreu's lives.

1

Simply Mary Smith

Mary Smith, more commonly known to the people as Miss MS, was 48 years old and an American citizen of English origin. Maybe her name sounds as common and as ordinary as any sullen and weary rainy morning. It was the first day of the working week on a nasty October Monday in 2013. New York City was being its coarse and unsociable self. From six o'clock in the morning shivering people were on their way to work illuminated by the watery glow of the street lights and car headlamps as they tried to dodge the rain and the slush thrown up by passing vehicles. Oh, that was a wet day.

And despite the woman having an ordinary and common name, plain Mary Smith, everything else about Mary Smith was extravagant – there was no doubt. Our singular lady was the richest woman in the USA and the owner of the world's most prosperous publishing company. Its capital flow was so vast that Miss S was jokingly referred to as Miss M$ or in speech as Miss D for all the juicy Dollars in her bank account.

An extraordinarily astute and determined businesswoman, she had created the Miss MS publishing at exactly the right time, producing books solely depending upon the market wants. Mary Smith had analyzed the readers' taste precisely and then produced books according to the exact liking of the consumers. From the simple birth of a book, she crafted number one bestsellers worldwide.

Miss MS Publishing's mission statement was simple: "Whatever you want, I'll give it to you. If you fancy a pair of astronauts making love inside a rocket, that's the story you can have it. Or if you prefer a woman being possessed by a Titan, we can give you that too. Absolutely everything you ask for shall be granted". Miss MS had simply created editorial to measure, the same as an "off the shelf tailored suit" but instead with books designed to the exact taste of the readers. No one understood how she had done it, as Mary Smith's professional secrets would be going with her to the grave, but what everyone knew was that everything this wise woman laid her hand on turned to gold. With her hidden strategies and deft marketing techniques, she had become the 'Queen Midas' of bestsellers all over the world.

Back in the 2010's, romance, erotic and pornographic books had become the most avidly consumed genres. The dark and depressing worldview that was fostered by the economic recession, the sharp decline of the dollar and the consequent decline in purchasing power, readers no longer wanted to read sad stories. Things were bad enough with their deplorable and pitiful lives, trying to make ends meet without having to read depressing or mournful stories. And there she was, Mary Smith providing them with the most beautiful love stories ever written.

As a matter of fact, Miss MS Publishing had just launched two romantic novels that hit 10 Million sales in less than two months. The first work by the famous writer "Orlando The Great" was the unforgettable love story between an American Army Captain and a European Lieutenant, where the love between them was so noble and great that it transcended borders, countries and cultures. The second work, by the less well known writer "Carmen Spain" hadn't shifted as many units, but its sales were slowly but steadily increasing. The plot of Spain's novel was a bit "unusual" in literary terms since it was based on two aliens disguised as humans, fornicating with abandon in every corner of the planet Earth. In short, Mary Smith simply produced the fiction that the public wanted. She wasn't bothered about the literary quality. The only thing she wanted to do was create purely commercial literature.

And ironically it was precisely in the genre of the romantic, erotic and pornographic where the cruel fact of Mary's personal existence laid. She, the wealthiest woman in America; she who had multiplied the sales of the most beautiful love stories ever written; she who had thousands of employees (editors, translators, bookbinders, distribution, publicity, sales and marketing staff) at her disposal; she, who personally took charge of all the reading and rereading of every novel before they were cast into the outside world as fulminated rays; she after three failed marriages was the last person in the world to know about "love". It was indeed ironic that a woman so ignorant about 'love matters' knew so well how to sell fiction about it and launch such a sublime concept of love into the world when she herself knew nothing about it.

It was for this reason that Mary Smith woke up moody on that stormy October Monday. She always woke up alone, because she never knew true love and she doubted if she ever were to find it. Her three marriages had gone from bad to worse. The first was to Richard Milton;

American by birth, but like Mary of English parents. They lasted only a year together, and then parted through irreconcilable differences. Her marriage to her second husband, Tomas Davis, failed after six months and the cause cited was Tom's sexual impotence, which, according to Mary Smith, he should have informed her about before the wedding. Her third relationship, this time with Simon Onfray (of French origin) lasted exactly one lunar month or 28 days, which was all the time it took for her to find him in bed with another woman.

After a couple of timid yawns, Mary arose naked and just as she did every morning, beheld the city of New York spread out in all its glory beneath her from the panoramic windows of her penthouse apartment. The view from her majestic building made her feel like the Queen of The Big Apple, but she was a lonely monarch. How repeatedly she had thought to her herself that she would give everything she had not to be alone. Mary Smith would give away her whole reign just for a few crumbs of affection. Despite these thoughts, she emerged - as usual - with almost divine splendor above the other poor and weak mortals, and felt as if she was reborn gloriously and dazzlingly; like Phoenix resurgent on its own ashes.

Entering the bathroom she admired the reflection of her naked body in the 16th century French bronze framed mirror, a gift from her third ex husband. Although she was 48 years old, she was still a stunner thanks to the two hours of strenuous exercise she undertook every day in her private gym. An hour in the morning before work and another hour in the afternoon or evening after work, every day except Sundays. Her body still bewitched men and she liked that. Mary Smith loved the way that men were perplexed when they met her in person and not only because she was both extremely rich and very clever, but also because of her blunt, direct and powerful beauty. Tall and slender, even if perhaps a little on the thin side her tawny blonde hair tumbled to her neck, as she was never a woman of exaggerated width or length. Her beautiful blue eyes were icy with a distant and unresponsive crystal shine.

From her rosy lips, she always spoke frankly and with a cynical coldness, perhaps as a result of her English education, but she never stopped being polite, correct and elegant. She understood the power she had over others and her words always penetrated people's heads; half orders, half challenges. Mary Smith was accustomed to giving commands. However, what she wasn't aware of was the power she had over men who were so easily aroused when they saw this "goddess of flesh".

She selected black sports pants, a white T-shirt and the first pair of trainers that she found in her wardrobe. Entering the gym from her bedroom, she leapt directly onto the treadmill with the intention of martyring her body on that rainy October Monday morning.

She was simply Mary Smith.

2
The farewell

A month earlier, on the Cuban coast, September 2013

In a state of mind that could only be described as total nostalgia, the young Andreu was sunbathing on the pearly white sand beach as the endless blue turquoise sea lapped at his feet. The enormous responsibility that his mother had just imposed on him without even seeking his agreement, rested on his shoulders like a heavy stone.

Andreu was the eldest of Socorro's four children. The family lived together in a modest house, thanks to years of hard work, for Andreu in the tobacco plantations and Socorro in the packing area of Nestlé. That house was the only possession that his drunkard father was unable to take from them.

Andreu had two sisters: Sarita 17, who kept house while Socorro was working and Jasmine 13, who was the darling of the family for her good conduct and excellent grades at school. They were the apples of Andreu's eyes, but - as in every decent home – there was Justin the "rebel" he was only nine years old, but it was he who orchestrated all the mischief within the Santa Rosa family with true mastery.

They all worshiped their eldest brother; he was seen as more as their substitute father than a sibling.

As a child, Andreu was mocked by his classmates. His 'nut like' skin and his soft green eyes with their hint of hazelnut, distinguished him from the rest of the class. His unusual combination of colors prompted a host of different nicknames, but eventually just one stuck. He was now a handsome young boy, but he was still known as Andreu, alias "Mocha" because of the color of his skin.

And Mocha enjoyed spending as much of his free time as possible with three people in particular: Benjamin, who was also affectionately nicknamed as "the never doer" because he never did his homework at school and as he grew older his behavior made his nick name ever more appropriate.

The second friend was Ivan – Andreu's neighbor and best friend- who had defended him on countless times from all those bullies who teased him at school. Ivan was known in Bayamo simply as the "mad" because his fights were as legendary in the city as his two meter height and powerful punches.

And last but not least, was Fernanda whose tanned skin was the wonder of all. Andreu and Fernanda's story went back to when they were teenagers and met at the entrance of a nearby bar. It must have been fate that brought them together, since both of them were searching for their alcoholic fathers. From that day onwards they became close friends and deep in their hearts they knew it was because their family backgrounds were so similar that it seemed as if fate had cut them from the same cloth. However mostly they shared that sad look lost in the horizon as they scanned the sea looking for a better life.

****

"I promised myself not to remember." He thought to himself. "But how can I do so when I only have to close my eyes for all these memories to come flooding back to me? How many times have I been in this very same place during those bohemian nights, with all my friends sitting around the campfire with a good bottle of rum, warming our throats as we sang the verses that liberated the feelings of our great troubadours like Silvio Rodríguez or the grandmaster Luis Eduardo Aute?

All this happened under the umbrella of the waxing full moon.

And while all these thoughts passed through Andreu's mind, the intensity of the Sun's heat forced him to sit up. He was about to leave, but his soul was anchored in those sands and this made him unable to move. He passionately wished that something extraordinary would happen so that it would derail the expectations everyone had put upon him.

And once again as if seduced by a nymph - his gaze was lost in the blue waves of the sea until his eyesight became clouded by a sensation even more pleasurable.

Delicate hands covered his eyes and playfully dodged all Andreu's attempts to capture them. It was a game or perhaps even a declaration of love, where both could be so close to each other, without transgressing the border of their friendship.

"Fernanda, is it you?" - Andreu asked.

"Of course it is me." She replies liberating his eyes "Or perhaps you were expecting someone else?"

He continued playing along.

"Oh yes. I was expecting a stunning blonde who had asked me to be here so she could have wild sex with me all night long."

"You're a fool Andreu."

And they laughed together for a while.

3
The perfection of Mary Smith

Mary Smith spent precisely 30 minutes on the treadmill. That was 30 minutes to the second, no more no less. She followed up with 400 sit-ups, precisely 200 for the upper stomach and then 200 for the lower stomach. It was then time for the exercise bike, which she rode, with absolute precision, as if it was a divine religious act, for 20 minutes. By now it was 7am and she had completed her morning workout. This was the signal for Mr. Aldo Rocamora, her butler to enter the private gym bearing her breakfast on a silver tray.

Mr. Rocamora, which was how she always addressed him, was unable to look directly into Mary Smith's eyes. He had perfectly assumed his role as not only Mary's butler, but also the eternal penitent of all his sins. She, however, always made a point of looking down her nose at Rocamora, the disrespectful gaze stating that she would never forgive his sins.

"Good morning, Mr. Rocamora." - She acknowledged his presence with an irritable tone.

"Good morning madam." – He answered keeping his gaze focused on the floor.

Like a Monday sacrament, the silver tray bore a glass of water with the juice of half a lemon, a glass of grapefruit juice, two slices of bread with low fat cheese, a boiled egg and a cup of decaffeinated coffee.

"Why not the grain bread this morning?" She enquired with a nervous twist of her lip. "I do not pay you to make mistakes, Mr. Rocamora."
"Excuse me ma'am." The butler apologized with certain light relief. "But seeing as today is the first Monday of the month, it is scheduled to be plain brown bread this morning and not the grain bread."
"I apologize." She answered moderating her disapproving tone "I was wrong and you are of course correct."
"That's alright Ma'am." He said with the color rising in his cheeks. "We all make mistakes." He lowered his gaze once more and repeated. "We all make mistakes, don't we?"

Mary took a sip of the lemon soured water and then, just as Rocamora was about to take his leave in order that she could enjoy her breakfast alone

"Mr. Rocamora." -She called as the butler turned back to face her. "I hope you don't take me the wrong way and allow my words to hurt you. You know I am very susceptible with my meals."

"I know, madam. Are you well this morning?" The butler inquired as Mary gave him a puzzled look.

"I am perfectly well, Mr. Rocamora." She replied before taking a sip of the decaffeinated coffee. "You may retire."

Having finished her breakfast, Mary Smith returned to the bathroom and stripped off her sportswear, standing in front of the mirror she looked attentively at her naked body. It was exactly ten minutes past seven.

Stretching out her arms into a cross-position she was horrified to discover a hint of sagging skin. "I should add weights to the exercise programme and more protein to my diet." She said to herself with a sigh. She loathed what she saw reflected in the mirror. She was no longer the young woman she once was, how she hated growing old.

"Two hours a day just isn't enough." She complained and then – as was her daily ritual – she entered the millionaire shower cubicle and let the pressured jets pound her body; busting cellulite, boosting her blood circulation and opening up her pores, a fountain of youth to maintain the youth of her skin.

Her daily irrigation took exactly 10 minutes and at 20 minutes past seven that morning that she rushed to her wardrobe, as organized as a shoe store.

There, arranged with military discipline hung her clothes. All her blouses and suit jackets were of equal lengths, but many different colors. Perfect, organized and cautious, Mary Smith's skirts were never too short or too long. Like her tawny blond hair —everything to do with her was so moderate. Her skirts for example were exactly right above the knee - not an inch more or less. That was Mary Smith.

With her sparkling crystal eyes, she coldly selected what she was going to wear on that morning. All the suits were cut the same, since they were all created by the same designer, but on that rainy October morning she had to choose the appropriate color.

Monday, plus Rain in October equals red.

Indeed, being a Monday, to many the most depressing day of the week, red would be the most appropriate to make an exuberant entrance into her publishing empire's headquarters, conveniently located on the first floor of the building. "Red will lift the spirits of the staff." Mary Smith asserted. "Today I shall increase sales. I will give our readers what they want. "

It was half past seven and so far Miss MS had chosen the red suit. Now she needed a suitable blouse so she perused the blouse section in her extensive walk-in wardrobe. Like the suits all the blouses were exactly the same all designed by the same couturier. Each notched and with mathematical precision hemmed the same length to the waist. She chose a coal black silk and decided therefore that it should be a pair of Christian Laboutin high heels that would finish her outfit, the black upper to match the blouse while the red sole complemented the suit.

It was 35 minutes past seven by the time she had finished dressing and as was buckling on the $1.5 billion Vacheron Constantin Tour de L'Ile wristwatch, Julio, her hairdresser, was knocking lightly on the door.

"May I come in?' requested the stylist in a submissive tone.

"Come in Julio." Mary Smith replied.

Julio, the best and most expensive stylist in New York, smoothed Mary's hair with his modern Figaro techniques until it was completely straight. By then it was 7: 45 AM. Julio left and Sarah the makeup artist came in. In less than five minutes, Sarah applied a light foundation to Mary's face, mascara and blue pencil around her eyes, a pink blush to her cheeks and a final sweet rosy touch to her lips.

It was 7: 55 AM and Mary Smith was now almost ready to make her headquarters entrance. A mild spray of pure musk, as Miss MS was not prone to any exaggeration; she entered the secret code on her personal elevator's keypad and placed an elegant black shod foot on the Persian rug that carpeted the cabin.

A feather light touch on the glowing number one and the elevator began its silent descent as it took its master to work.

It was exactly 7:59 AM. At eight o'clock Mary Smith, with surgical precision, strode out of the elevator into the heart of her business empire.

4
The love in your eyes

City of Bayamo, Cuba, September 2013

Andreu's great reception on that afternoon had not been expected, but it could not been otherwise, given that he was such an adored person in the neighborhood. He attempted to enjoy the gathering with all his senses, as it would be his final party in his beloved Cuba. Early in the morning of the following he would be boarding the flight that would take him to where the American Dream is always brewing.

Before the unexpected party, Andreu had gone to say goodbye to Doña Catita. A septuagenarian, Doña Catita had been helping him for years. At dawn before he went to the tobacco plantation, Andreu had voluntarily assisted her at her stand. Doña Catita was the widow of a soldier who had died in a street fight and left her helpless, without any pension since he had never divorced his first wife. The good woman had been generous to the young Andreu wanting to give the street boys a "reason for living" on her pitiful wages she had bought sport uniforms for each and every one of 23 young boys who she then taught the basics of baseball, her favorite sport. This was how Andreu had learned to play baseball, thanks to the generosity of Dona Catita.

So in short Andréu was not only an attractive young boy because of the way he looked, and with which he seduced all the girls in his path, but also because of his kindness in providing help to all those who needed it, just like Doña Catita, who had helped him in return become the greatest baseball player in Bayamo.

After the surprise party, Andréu sat on the porch saying goodbye to all the friends. They all wished him the best of luck and more than one of them joked that he should never forget his poor friends back home when he became famous. The last one to speak to him was Fernanda who was his best friend forever.

"Another beer, Andreu?"
"No. Thanks." He replied. "I've had enough."
"Not enough." She said. "I can see you're still nervous."

To such an obvious statement he had no choice but to answer. They remained on the porch for a long time watching the coming and going of passers by until every one of the beer bottles were empty.

"I was waiting for people to leave us alone, Fernanda, so that I could tell you all the things that I have never dared to say before."

Almost involuntarily she interrupted him.

'Don't tell me Andreu please don't tell me. I convinced myself from that day I first watched you playing baseball on the field that if you ever had the opportunity to leave this island and become someone important, I would do anything to help you to achieve your dreams. But if you tell me what I want to hear all of my effort and determination for you to succeed will succumb to your desires, because they are also mine."

"No Fernanda. I don't want to remain silent. It's been about a year since that gringo came to me with the proposal to get me that athletic scholarship. The price was high: to go to LA and leave my life here behind. At first it was like seeing all my efforts finally rewarded. For weeks I believed I was living in a dream, everything was perfect. But as time passed, I became convinced that even though everyone was encouraging me that I shouldn't leave because of you. It is not my other friends or relatives who are stopping me leaving, it's you. I know that if I work hard I'll make it and I can come back home and give all my brothers here in Cuba what they can't have now. But you are the deepest root for me. Your smile, your honey colored eyes and the sweet smell of your skin that follows me every day and everywhere. Just ask me and I will stay here with you forever."

She broke into tears at such tender words.

"You are the greatest of fools Andreu. How could it take you so long to realize what you feel for me? I have always felt it for you. Now I am not the one who asks you, but begs you to leave because I know that if I keep you with me, you will regret it for every day of the rest of your life."

Without saying a further word she got up and ran off without looking back at him.

The next day at the airport Andreu desperately sought out Fernanda, his confidante, her love the only thing that would keep him in that little island, but she never showed up. The roar of the engines was the blade that separated the two lovers from their beautiful love.

She was staring at the sky as it was crossed by Andreu's plane. Each of them was holding on to an identical bracelet that Fernanda had woven as a symbol of their great friendship.

The sky, a plane and two souls united by a great love.

And two tears streaming down their cheeks.

5
The headquarters

At bang on 9am the elevator doors opened. Margaret, Mary Smith's secretary, was waiting for her expectantly. Mary Smith strode into the lobby with her characteristic imposing and serious gait as Margaret rushed to keep up with her.

"Good day." The immaculately groomed Margaret greeted her boss.
"Good Morning Margaret." Mary Smith replied with her heels clicking along the corridor towards her office.
"What's new today?"
"I've phoned Orlando The Great a short while ago. He says that he refuses to keep on writing for us unless we

raise his cut of the profits from 5 per cent to 10 per cent," Margaret answered pensively.

"Very Well." Mary Smith snorted haughtily. "Tell him not to bother writing anything more for us." She added wryly. "He is not going to play with me. Who does he think he is? He should go and see whether he can find another publisher who can give him 10 per cent."

"Fair enough." Margaret replied with a wry smile. She had been working for Mary Smith for many years now and was familiar with her brutal honesty.

Obediently Margaret returned to her office to call Orlando The Great as Mary Smith lowered herself into the swivel chair behind her antique desk, her back and shoulders held straight.

Back upstairs in Mary Smith's apartment, Mr. Rocamora was picking up the discarded nightwear and sports clothes scattered on the marble floor of the bedroom and bathroom. He gathered the wet towels together and once everything was exactly how his lady liked it - he went to the kitchen to prepare her lunch and dinner. At exactly 12:30 he would place the meal with its meticulously calculated calorie content on the silver tray and call the elevator and ride down to the first floor with it. On his return to the kitchen the pre-prepared dinner would be left for Mary smith to warm up after work. With all his tasks completed Mr. Rocamora could retire to his home for a rest.

Mary Smith arose from her chair, walked to the full length mirror mounted on the back of the office door and examined her reflection once again - - the memory of those "hanging wings" from her upper arms itched at her thoughts. She was getting hopelessly old ... yeah ... but she was still as stiff as a bullet. Her breasts were still beautiful, though that perfection came courtesy of the famous Iranian specialist, Dr. Masoud Dastgerdi, who had also ironed out the wrinkles on her forehead and the cellulite on her thighs. "But what about those damned wrinkles on my neck tracking down to my collar bones?" She sighed wearily.

Her skin was still perfect. She had abundant blond hair, which perfectly framed the expertly made-up beauty of her face, but her hands were no longer so admirable, like her neck the dry skin was beginning to become lined and cracked.

"Tired old me!" She concluded before returning to her throne like a solitary monarch. "How difficult it is to keep my image frozen in time!"

A knock on the door interrupted her thoughts. It was Margaret.

"Come in." Barked Mary Smith.
"The writer known as Orlando The Great has informed me that ... " Margaret paused and sank to her knees.
"What did he say?" Mary Smith asked a slight smile curling her lips in anticipation of the writer's response. "Repeat to me word for word what he said."
"Yes Miss Smith." Margaret cast an evasive look around her; just to be sure no one else was in the office. "He said you can go to hell."

A strange silence descended between the two women. Margaret's face had reddened while Mary Margaret Smith looked as stiff as a starched shirt.

"How curious!" Mary Smith snapped. "It is certainly interesting to note how originally writers can express themselves sometimes." The tone of her voice rose audibly. "But who does he think he is, that cheesy writer?" she shouted. "He's a ridiculous and annoying writer."
"Yes Miss." Margaret agreed stunned by the violence of Mary Smith's reaction.

"Well then, what's the plan for today?" A calmer Mary Smith immediately changed the subject.

"The male models are coming over for the book jacket photoshoot. They will be in reception at twelve-thirty. Here are the reference photos." Margaret placed the folder of images on Mary's desk.

"OK. Tell Mr. Rocamora then he should leave the tray on my desk." Mary instructed Margaret.

"Yes Miss." Margaret hesitated to ask. "But what shall I do with the Orlando The Great?"

Mary Smith scratched her chin several times before saying:

"It's very simple. Tell him to fuck off back to hell too."

Mary Smith was amazed at her own words. She hadn't sworn for many a year, but the truth of the matter was that she found it cathartic. Her outburst made her feel better, much better.

"No, just tell him to fuck off." She concluded.

6
The American dream

Andreu had to keep looking at the seat number 138, printed on his boarding pass, for it to register in his brain that he was finally leaving behind the sunny days of his beloved Cuba.

Cautiously he walked down the aisle before settling into his assigned seat next the window.

His fear was evident in the persistent rubbing of his palms against the fabric of his trouser legs to wipe away the sweat.

Takeoff was tortuous: the initial vibration and then the rising noise of the aircraft engines made him think that everything around him was going to collapse.

Once in the air his body regained a measure of composure and his innocent curiosity of the unknown future awaiting him began to play in his imagination. Constantly stroking the only tangible symbol he possessed of his love for Fernanda: the woven bracelet, it brought back to him some of the indelible moments that were inscribed in his memory.

****

The irritating whistle of his friend "The Never Doer" announced to Andreu's ears that it was time to leave for the baseball field, where all the neighborhood kids were waiting for the regular Sunday amateur league game. Andreu was the team captain and pitcher.

Andreu quickly put those books away on an old shelf as destiny had given him the opportunity to resume to his medical career.

Doña Catita's donations - old and faded - were taken quickly by Andreu and without a second thought he rushed out of the house and got into Ivan's old Cadillac 51.

"Quickly." The two meter giant cried. "Do you want us to be disqualified for your tardiness?"
"Do not despair, my friend. I lost track of the time studying."
'You will never change." The Never Doer interrupted.
"If it is not a pretty face, it is your books, there is always something that slows you down."

The old Cadillac rolled down the narrow island alleys until reaching the old once abandoned baseball field.

Now it was once again at its peak thanks to Doña Catita and her baseball team. They were in the semifinals.

****

The ball came to and went - with dizzying speed – from Andreu's vigorous hand. His refined and effective throw outlining prodigious curves and straights only visible to the eyes of the adoring fans surrounding the field.

On the road approaching the field an old Russian built Lada, was slowly getting closer. Compared with the vintage American automobiles it was cramped, but it still complied with its function as a taxi. Inside a lone American was on his way to his hotel. His presence on the island was just a simple holiday, but one, which he had postponed due his wife's lost six month battle with leukemia.

****

"Robert, promise me that you will go when I leave." A cough interrupted the woman's flow of conversation from the hospital bed. "Swear that when all this is over you will take that trip that you promised me."

The middle-aged man, trying to remain positive in front of his wife replied:

"But what are you saying? You'll see that in a few days you will be so healthy that we will both take that long-deserved vacation to Cuba. We just have to wait for the new medication to work."

She took his hand smiling at his little deception.

"Whatever you say Robert."

****

Now Robert was fulfilling the promise that he had made to his beloved wife.

"Excuse me sir, what is that place?" Robert inquired curiously.
"You mean where all those people are?" The driver asked.

The taxi driver who understood some English – thanks to the constant influx of tourists to the island - knew immediately what that question was about.

"It's the old Bayamo baseball field. Today is the semifinals and the truth is that it is said that our Pitcher is the best thing that has been seen here in many years." The driver assured the American inflating his chest with pride.

"Stop please." Robert replied enthusiastically.

"Did I say something to upset you sir?" The cabbie was bewildered.

"On the contrary my friend, quite the opposite."

He took a twenty-dollar bill from his wallet and paid off the driver leaving him with a large tip.

Robert took a seat in one of the upper tiers, which is from where you can best appreciate the game – as if the players were chess pieces – there Robert now discovered that the words of the taxi driver were entirely true. Andreu was throwing the ball again and again. His opponents marched off one after another without being able to hit a single one of his bowls. It was almost as if they were 'ghost balls'. The game ended with a narrow victory for Bayamo, placing them in the finals.

****

Sarita was busy with her chores when a few sharp raps on the door interrupted her. She opened the door and was surprised to find that the visitor was not one of her usual home guests.

"What you want?"

In a shady Spanish the unknown but obviously foreign man tried to communicate with the girl.

"Me llamo Robert, Robert Maqueda, y mi hablar con tu hermano."
'You mean Andreu?" Sarita replied in English. "And can you tell why you are looking for him?"
"Hablar de job ... dinero." Robert was sweating.
"I understand. You mean job, right?" Sarita said shrewdly.
"That's right, my trabajou."
"Well mister, what does your work have to do with my brother?"
"If you let me in. "Robert said, pointing into the house.
"Forgive my rudeness. Please come in."

Once in the house Sarita offered Robert a glass of cold orange juice diluted with water. Andreu's mother joined them in the room. After a great effort Robert was able to make them understand that his interest in Andreu was to take him back to the United States of America to play baseball in a team in California.

The matron of the Santa Rosa family could only mutter words of gratitude for Robert. In her eyes he was like an angel fallen from heaven. In the solitude of his room - again and again - Andreu tried to put everything into perspective. He could not help wondering if what was happening could be true.

It had been a strange twist of fate that had brought Robert to stop and witness one of his best games. This was a man who was one of the baseball coaches at the most prestigious university in California, whose name in English Andreu had still not succeeded in pronouncing yet.

7
A Cuban in Los Angeles

The pilot informed them that they were about to land at Los Angeles International Airport, known simply as LAX, all around him sleepy passengers stirred from their lethargy to buckle up their seat belts. Andreu was very tired, because of American restrictions on flights from

Cuba he'd had to spend the night at Cancun in Mexico, before catching his connection to LAX.

When the plane finally put down on the tarmac and Andreu descended into the airport, he was surprised to see how those Americans, who only a few days earlier had been enjoying the lazy pace of Cuba, were now frantically rushing about as if driven by the desire to overcome time itself.

He scanned the airport with his eyes and what he saw amazed him. LAX was far from what he had imagined. The architecture of the airport was so huge and imposing to him that it seemed worthy of admiration.

Having cleared Immigration and Customs he made his way to the exit. The cars he saw on the streets did not look like the vintage American cruisers and old Soviet models back at home. In Havana, people walked slowly admiring the sea while the warm breeze cooled down their damp skins. But there, everything in his path was so different. In Cuba he could only dream of being next to something as luxurious as a brand new Porche or Bugatti, he had only ever seen those on postcards or in magazines, but now he was just a few yards away from them. He could not resist the temptation to caress the

Bugatti Veyron parked by his side, without realizing what was about to happen.

"Hey what're you doing man?" came a voice from behind.

When he turned the light reflected off the mirror shades of a young blonde boy, whose outfit was completed by boots, jeans and a casual shirt with the logo of a moose.

"Quiet friend, I was just admiring how nice your car is. Just that." Andreu answered uneasily.
"Mother Fucker." Added the American.

At this time Andreu did not know the English language very well, but his limited knowledge was sufficient to understand such an international word.

The chances that the flimsy boy, who was probably accustomed to a life of pampered luxury, could overcome the muscular Cuban youth were negligible. Andreu was used to working ten hours shifts under the scorching sun in the Cuban tobacco plantations.

So when the American pushed Andreu he didn't think twice. He punched him in the face and then followed with a left to the chin. The American went down immediately. It was at that moment that Robert appeared at the scene. He'd witnessed what had happened from the opposite side of the road, and understood perfectly well that Andreu's hot blood would lead to trouble if he were swayed by his temperament.

"Easy Boy, easy." Robert said to Andreu as he grabbed him by the arm. "But He is KO'd. Oh my God!"

8
Mary Smith and the dark-haired men

With the precision of a Swiss watch, at exactly 12:30 PM, Mary Smith was seated the meeting room on the ground of her building. To her right was Margaret her secretary, and on her left was her Marketing Director, Elena Rubeyenski.

Mr. Rocamora had already left the silver tray with a glass of water with the juice of half a lemon; a lettuce, celery and cucumber salad dressed with lemon and fresh mint. Two pieces of low calorie Feta cheese with toasted bread, an apple and an herbal tea.

Mary Smith took a quick glance at the food. It seemed to be correct for the first Monday of every month.

As Mary Smith began to sip from the glass of water with the lemon juice, it was the first thing that she always took before any meal; a file of 100 men entered the room in single file. Some were youths and some more mature, chosen to appeal to the needs of different markets. On that particular day three male models were required for three book jackets due to be launched into the market by Christmas 2013.

The books were entitled *Warriors Love, Love In The Clouds*, and the third *On A Deserted Island*.

Mary Smith knew how important an excellent jacket was for selling books. Sometimes readers bought more with their eyes than with any other sense and a handsome specimen of masculinity on the cover, would provide that extra push to encourage consumers to buy.

Mary immediately began to eat the salad while carefully examining each of the men crowded into the room. As she expected lurking in the corners were the shyest, while the most confident occupied the middle ground.

"All Right. Thank you all for coming." Elena's voice amplified by the bullhorn she favored for such events echoed around the room pounding the brains of the assemble throng to jelly like the pounding of a hammer.

Then she whispered into Mary Smith's ear. "Shall we start with the model for *Warriors Love*?" Miss MS nodded and continued munching on her salad.

"All Right. We shall commence with the redheads." Elena yelled through the bullhorn. "Since the hero of our first novel *Warriors Love* is a redhead, we therefore need all you redheads to take a step forward. I repeat, only the redheads, please."

Out of the 100 assembled, 35 stepped forward.

"And now." Elena said addressing the 35 red headed men. "Remove your shirts please and then very slowly sashay along the catwalk towards us. When you arrive in front of us, keep still, until we tell you to leave. Doe anyone have any questions?"

The 35 red headed men remained silent.

One by one they paraded down the cat walk. Their footsteps echoed metallically as if they were a troop of soldiers. By the time they were lined up in front of the panel, Mary Smith had finished the salad and was munching on the cheese-topped toast.

"What do you think?" Mary Smith asked Margaret.
"I don't like any of them. Sure the hero of *Warriors Love* is a redhead, but he is also a Celt. None of these men seem to have the look of an ancient Celtic warrior." Margaret voiced her true opinion.
'And what do you think?" Mary Smith passed the question to Elena.
"I'm not convinced by any of them." Elena said cutting straight to the point.
"Then cast then all aside and find some other Celtic warrior redheads." Mary said forcefully and took a sip of her herbal tea.

The redheaded men trooped out of the room, and now it was the turn of the 40 flaxen blonde haired men to parade down the catwalk. The novel, *Love In The Clouds*, was about a pair of spirits who loved each other like angels. This time they had more luck finally selecting Johnny a young ruddy boy with velvety skin who looked as if he had just descended from heaven. He was perfect for the cover of *Love In The Clouds*.

The blondes were ushered out of the room and it was now the turn of the dark haired men to take to the cat walk for the cover the third book, *On A Deserted Island*. By the time they were ready Mary Smith had dropped the core of her apple onto the silver platter.

So 25 men with flawless olive skins paraded down the catwalk and Mary Smith enjoyed the show. These were her kind of men and it secretly excited her. This was one of her hidden tastes -intimate and unconfessed- but for her inevitable. Mary Smith found herself once more aroused by tanned skins and hot bodies.

As they came and went, displaying their fiery olive skins, Mary Smith gently stroked her right thigh. Then with her left hand she slowly caressed her neck before subconsciously covering her mouth – as if to prevent her secret thoughts from escaping into to the world.

"Oh." She said to herself. "I wish I had eaten one of those olives, instead of Mr. Rocamora's lunch."

Then she shook her head violently to focus her mind back on the job in hand.

9
Sigma, Alpha, Epsilon

Late September 2013, University of Southern California

Robert had, with a wealth of details, explained to Andreu the promising future that was within his grasp, as long as he was willing to pay a high price. On his very first freshman day he joined America's most legendary baseball team: the Trojans, who throughout their career had won more than 100 national titles.

During training, Andreu won, with relative ease, two good friends, Johan and Patrick, with whom he was also to share a room.

Johan and Patrick differed from one another like "oil and water". Johan appeared to be a quiet, studious boy who came from a vastly wealthy family, despite Johan's father having lost much of his fortune through gambling. The family still hung on to some valuable properties, including a residence in central New York - a vestige of the glamour of their social class. Conversely, Patrick came from suburban New Jersey and enjoyed a life of total freedom. He did not care that his parents exerted pressure on him to get the best results- he just did what he pleased.

****

It was the last Friday of November 2013 and Johan and Andreu were revising for their end of term exams. They were both engrossed in their studies when Patrick euphorically entered the room, to remind them of the great festival to be held in the Fraternity.

"Damn, I forgot it was today." Johan said. "You're coming, aren't you?" He asked Andreu.
"Thanks for the invitation, but I don't think it's a good idea to go. I don't belong to the Brotherhood." Andreu replied his nose fixed deep inside a medical text book.
"Does it matter?" Patrick protested.
"Come on Cuban." Johan added.

At the insistence of his friends Andreu agreed to go, knowing that his mind also could do with a short break.

The noise of the party could be heard from a few blocks away. Alcohol ran freely through the house and the most beautiful girls on campus were also present. Everyone knew it was one of the best celebrations of the year. Of course, the most revered member of the Fraternity was there too, Marcus, the leader and captain of the Trojans.

Laughter, alcohol and pretty girls, kept the three friends happy. It was Johan's power of observation that detected the insistent gaze of one of the union members of the Sigma Alpha Epsilon Fraternity. The guy fixed his eyes on Andreu – but not very favorably. Johan cautiously asked Andreu to help him get some beers from the bar counter.

"Listen to me Andreu." Johan whispered into his ear once they reached the bar counter. "Do you see that guy over there? He is a second year student and his name is Joshua."
"Yes, I see him now." Andreu said with a shrug of his shoulders.
"Now take your eyes off him. It is not a good thing to have him as your enemy." Johan slowly explained.
"Who is this Joshua?" Andreu was intrigued, paying full attention to his friend's words.
"He's a nobody, but the important thing is that he is Marcus' younger brother. Now you know what I mean, don't you?" Johan winked at Andreu. "If you have

problems with Joshua, you'll have problems with Marcus and his whole legion of gorillas."

"No worries, my friend." replied Andreu. "I will try not to cross his path and now let's stop all this nonsense and continue enjoying the party. You brought me here with the promise of a good hangover tomorrow and I'm not leaving this place without fulfilling that promise."

****

It was nearly three o'clock in the morning by the time the party was over and the three friends decided to return to their rooms. Feeling rather tipsy they soon sobered up when they heard a van stop behind them. The wheels squealed noisily leaving long tracks on the asphalt. Fifteen burly young men spilled out of the van behind them. Out of the fifteen, one of them stood out and it was Joshua.

"Do you remember me Cuban?" Joshua shouted at Andreu.

Andreu tried to focus his gaze on the young man before him and chill ran down his spine; suddenly he understood why all this was happening. His mind flashbacked to his first day in Los Angeles and he remembered the rich punk in the mirror shades.

"Ah you're the idiot from the airport." Andreu started laughing uncontrollably. "I don't think you've taken the trouble to come all the way here just to ask me to dance with you, honey?"
"Shut up Andreu." Johan hissed at Andreu, as Joshua's temper bristled by the second.
"But what are you saying Johan? These are a just a bunch of pimps." El Cubano added with his fiery Latin blood up.

Before he could say anything Patrick was silenced with a strong punch to the head.

"You better shut your big Cuban mouth." Continued Joshua. "If you don't want your friends to pay for your insolence."
"They have nothing to do with this." Andreu was furious. "Let them go. This is just between you and me."
"OK that's fair enough and you see I'm a generous guy. I will let them go. But you have to stay right here for this private party that we've organized for you."
"And you know what's the best part will be?" Andreu spat through grinding teeth.

"What?" replied Joshua his face splitting into a rictus grin.
"That you are going to be my bitch all night." Concluded Andreu as he lashed out his fury towards Joshua.

Joshua's fifteen thugs drew into a circle around Andreu allowing Johan and Patrick to draw back a few meters beyond them.

"What shall we do Johan?" Patrick asked.
"I don't know. If we go back they will grind us to pieces, not to mention that we'll have the entire fraternity pitched against us, but we can't just leave him on his own."
"What shall we do?" Patrick repeated.
"Fuck it let's join in." Johan screamed with all his might.
"Why?" Patrick asked.
"So we'll have something to tell our kids when we get older." Johan growled.

Andreu smiled when he saw them coming back. The battle was going to be simply epic.

10
The bird in the golden cage

Meanwhile the solitary Mary Smith was wandering through the empty corridors of her building, with fourteen floors her majestic building had a lot space for Mary's late night prowling. Occasionally she bumped into one of the security officers, there were two stationed on each floor. Each one greeted her politely making a small gesture of reverence by doffing their caps. Mary just waved back to them with a slight rise of her right hand. It was three o'clock in the morning and while Andreu and his friends were handing out the greatest beating of their lives, Mary Smith continued her journey through the deserted corridors of her building, her blue crystal irises gazing ahead into the distance and occasionally pinching her thigh, digging her nails into her flesh.

She meandered from floor to floor, pretending that she had absolute control over herself and her actions, and the truth of it was that this was the best of her strategies. That night she could not sleep. To the outside world she presented herself as a lucid woman with a deeply organized mind, but on the inside she was filled with self-doubt and anxiety. And sometimes, only sometimes, she had to pinch her own thighs until they bled just as she was doing at that very moment to stop herself from crying. Mary Smith was really lonely.

That afternoon Mr. Rocamora had collected the tray from where she had left it and taken the elevator back up to her penthouse in order to prepare her final meal for the day. Once done his workday was over and before he left that Friday he ensured that each object was exactly where it had to be, just where she wanted it to be. Every object had its own correct place and its precise location was part of the function for each single object in her mind. Nothing must vary from that mathematical order. For a brief moment he felt some sympathy for her. Mr. Rocamora regarded her as a bird in a golden cage. Before he left for the evening he slowly checked the position of each and every object. He was paid to be her butler. He was not paid to think for himself or pay for his past sins.

That Friday in November 2013, nothing out of the ordinary had happened to Mary Smith, it was just like any other Friday of the year. Thankfully following a heated telephone exchange between Orlando the Great and Margaret, Orlando had finally backed down and accepted a seven per cent cut of the profits, which was actually what Mary Smith had planned from the very beginning.

After spending many hours roaming around the labyrinthine maze of corridors in her building, Mary Smith retired to her penthouse. Mr. Rocamora had left her ready prepared dinner on the tray, but she hadn't touched it. It was three-thirty in the morning by then and she could not eat or sleep. She examined the food intently: A glass of water with the juice of half a lemon, tofu tortilla, steamed vegetables with a dressing of olive oil, a fruit salad and a glass of red wine.

Mary Smith's meticulous mind agreed that that was the correct menu, but could not open her mouth. She hadn't felt that lonely for a long, long time.

11
Marcus' revenge

The altercation between Joshua and Andreu soon reached the attention of Marcus, who would not let any Cuban upstart destroy his own little kingdom.

"Well what have you found out about the Cuban?" Marcus questioned one of his lieutenants with characteristic authority.
"Not much." Answered the minion. "He is in the fourth year of a medicine degree. His grades are good and he's

on the University baseball team. I don't understand how you have not run into him in the changing rooms."

"So how come he's a just arrived from Cuba three months ago and already in the fourth year of medical school and in the baseball?" Marcus inquired incredulously.

"Robert." The henchman shrugged as he answered.

"Robert, the coach of the baseball team?" Marcus enquired opening his eyes wide with curiosity.

"Robert saw him play baseball when he was on his Cuban vacation and he liked his game. Robert offered him the opportunity to come to the United States on a scholarship and Andreu was already at med school in Cuba so he went straight into year four. You must have heard about the legendary medical cover in Cuba."

"It's True." Confirmed Marcus. "They are a superpower when it comes to medical advancement. Their government invests a significant amount of the national budget on the health of its citizens."

"He has a scholarship." Marcus' minion added. "And on top of all that, he doesn't seem to have any problems with his passport or visas. Incredibly he has been granted with an "indefinite" visa."

"Damn." Marcus mumbled. "He must have "something" that we can use against him."

"Well I don't think so. The guy is pretty quiet. No drugs, no alcohol and no mess with women. He is too damned clean." The spy replied and stopped to think. "But if I find something else, I'll inform you."

"And what are you waiting for? Think." Marcus yelled as he lost his control.

"Oh well, there is only one thing I can think of. His university registration does not indicate a known address in this country."

"Explain yourself before I lose my patience." Marcus hissed.

"Well the guy came directly from Cuba and he is on a scholarship which was processed by Robert, and as I said, he has a permanent visa."

"All Right then. Now that's useful information. We'll just have to push the Cuban a little and he may lose his scholarship." Marcus grinned. "In the meantime, tell the boys to get ready, we are going to pay a visit to those three."

***

Immersed in the shadows, the Sigma Alpha Epsilon goons were waiting for the lights in Andreu's rooms to go out. Shrouded by the darkness, they infiltrated the building and seized Andreu and his two friends.

Blindfolded and with their hands and feet bound with cable ties, the three were taken to the outskirts of the campus, where the fraternity initiation techniques were normally carried out.

"I am pleased to meet you, Cuban. I know that I need to introduce myself and tell you the reasons why you are here in ... " Marcus made a short pause for effect and grinned... "Big shit."
"Why don't we settle this like men, just between you and me, Marcus?" Andreu answered.
"And miss out all the fun? No. This is just the beginning for you and these two traitors who beat up my brother and his friends. Punishment is a must and for the rest of the semester."

Andreu, Johan and Patrick were thrown into the pond still with their hands tied and forced to swim throughout the night using only their legs. Marcus' orders were met with exacting rigor; all three of them were driven to the verge of collapse, but despite the harsh punishment, not one of them complained.

It was in this manner that they spent the month of December 2013, where the long list of daily punishments and humiliations began to wear them down.

"This can't continue. We should go and confront them once and for all." Patrick said sullenly as he threw a plastic Christmas bauble against the bedroom wall. "So we continue being punished until we graduate?" Johan responded as he picked the bauble off the floor. "For once in your life think first before you talk."

However, Andreu was in more trouble than his two friends, especially since Robert was about to withdraw his support if Andreu's game kept declining.

"There's only one way out of this impasse." Andreu interrupted.

And without another word he got up and walked out of the door. That day was 31st December 2013.

12
Sweet Christmas

So after November came December. Sales at Miss MS Publishing had risen prodigiously. Mary Smith was a lynx, a winner; the richest and most powerful woman in the United States of America, but her bedroom continued to be cold and silent - dripping loneliness.

"How many people envy you?" She wondered to herself using her ability to split her personality into two halves. "Everybody." She responded to herself and she began to find it difficult to breath as her throat dried out.
"Do they understand your sorrow?"
"No. Nobody knows anything about it."

The arrival of thousands of Christmas cards had interrupted her thoughts. They flooded her perfect minimalist living room making it look totally disorganized. The thousands of Christmas greetings annoyed her as much as a persistent buzzing of a fly. All of her employees had sent her one: from the cleaning operatives to the marketing department. Each of workers at the fourteen Miss MS Publishing printing and distribution plants had sent her the common Christmas card with soothes rudimentary and boring words.

"Merry Christmas Miss MS."
"Merry Christmas and Happy New Year."

It was the time of the year that everyone called the "period of joy" where drinking, laughing and partying were indulged in by all and there she was trying to find some meaning in her life.

How sad, her existence was passing by without having loved or been loved!

Once she had calmed herself she opened the blinds and gazed out of her window, overlooking the festivity field that was New York City, she blinked and compressed her lips into a thin line.

"How many hours are left of the Old Year?" She asked herself angrily.
"No idea. Perhaps in less than an hour it will be 2014. I don't know why these damned hours preceding the New Year seem to take so long and are accompanied by this annoying silence. I wish that it is already January and I can go back to work. I want it to be morning and then at least I can see my three ex-husbands, like I do every year."
"Why?" She asked herself ironically and with any fear of anticipating the answer in advance.
"Because I want to go to sleep and wake up on a clear day where I can forget that I'm all alone." She shrugged her shoulders as she lied to herself.

"You damned fool. You are a solitary wolf." She repeated to herself in a fatigued tone. "Tonight you shall return to the coldness of your sheets. Nobody will be there at your side. Poor little Miss Mary Smith. You are an aimless soul. You were born alone and you will die alone."

The clock struck twelve. It was now January 1st 2014. Merry Christmas and a Happy New Year Miss Mary Smith.

****

Meanwhile on the campus of the University of Southern California...

"Marcus, Marcus." Andreu defiantly shouted outside the house of the Trojans.

Marcus burst out of the doors followed by all his retinue; he bristled with arrogance and power.

"Who do you think you are Cuban to come to my house and scream at me in that way?"
"Do you think you are a brave guy?" Andreu shouted violently back. "What are you afraid of Marcus? Huh?

Are you afraid that I will leave you face the same as I did to that jerk of that brother of yours?" Andreu's blood was boiling.

Marcus lunged forward, stabbing his pointed finger at Andreu.

"If this is what you want, I'll gladly give it to you." Marcus said from behind gritted teeth.
"Come on right here and show me what you've got. " Andreu invited him forward with a gesture of his fingers.
"Not here." Marcus replied coldly as the twelve chimes announcing the New Year rang out. "There's an abandoned place two miles from here. Let's finish this there." Come on then." Andreu agreed and put down his raised fists.

As the van engines revved up Marcus beckoned over one of his minions "Don't forget to bring the video camera I'm going to want to see this again."

Arriving at the clearing Marcus yelled "You're screwed Cuban. Before adding Come on has fear paralyzed your legs?"
"I'll break your face like I did to your sister." Andreu riposted.

Marcus rushed towards Andreu and grappled him. The Cuban squirmed like a viper trying to free himself from the bigger and stronger man. The blows they exchanged to their faces wet the dry surface of the abandoned clearing with their blood. For minutes it seemed that they were evenly matched, but Andreu's uncontrollable rage came to the fore and a hard right punch to Marcus' face landed Andreu the victory.

If only Marcus had intended to fulfill the agreement between the pair of them it would have been the end of Andreu's problems with the fraternity of Alpha Epsilon Sigma.

13
The Paparazzi (first part)

1st January 2014

Mary Smith woke up that morning feeling much happier. Although her office was still closed for the Christmas holidays, she would soon be able to get back to something like normal activity. Moreover, she had her usual New Year's appointments with her three former husbands as had become customary over the years. First, at nine am she would have breakfast with the first of the ex-husbands, Richard Milton, in the Atelier at the Ritz-Carlton in Central Park. After that, at 12:30 pm, she would take lunch with her second former husband and finally at 6:30 pm she was going to dine with Simon Onfray, her third former husband at Alain Ducasse's Essex House Restaurant.

This had been her practice since her third divorce for one sole reason: the meetings provided excellent publicity for the four of them splashing their images over the covers of all the newspapers and the celebrity and gossip magazine. The headline would run "Mary Smith reunites with her three ex-husbands for New Year celebrations."

****

Mary Smith arrived at the Atelier in her white Bentley Flying Spur limousine and as always there was Richard ready to open the door for her. Richard, an American but of English origin, knew exactly how to treat everyone with politeness even his ex-wife. Mary Smith thanked him and slowly ran her eyes over his body as he held the Bentley's door open. With his short blond hair and blue eyes, he was neither handsome nor ugly. In short, nothing in his way cried out for attention except for his taste for elegantly tailored suits.

"You are late." Richard admonished her.
"No. I am never late. It is exactly nine o'clock."
"I'm sorry dear. It is three minutes past nine." He corrected her.
"As accurate as always." Mary spat through gritted teeth.
"Not as accurate as you, my dear." Richard replied with an arch of an eyebrow.
'Go to hell, my love." She replied with one of her most dazzling smiles.

Inside the restaurant as they took their table for breakfast a couple of paparazzi started to shoot pictures. The Maitre'D had them politely ushered out back on the street.

"Oh you are still so picky." She rebuked him while taking a quick look at the menu.
"And you are so perfect." Richard said watching her intently. "Our relationship might have worked if you had not been so perfect, but we only had a brief relationship."
"Yes. We lasted only for a year." She said and then ordered everything she fancied from the French menu;

since New Year's Day was the only day she ever skipped her diet.

"No dear." He contradicted her again. "We lasted exactly one year and ten days."

"What I don't understand is how we lasted that long. You continue to be unbearable even now." She replied

As stiff as statue, the waiter stared at the ceiling pretending not to have heard their exchange as he took down their choices.

Breakfast over; they left the Atelier in complete apathy, as they had been done for the previous twenty years since their divorce. The paparazzi's pictures had been taken and wired to the news desks as the breakfast farce was concluded until the following year.

"Happy New Year, Miss Mary Smith." Richard said with his characteristic arch of a blond eyebrow.
"The same to you." She replied keeping her back to him.

And the two of them went their own ways. On the way back home perched on the red leather upholstery of the white Bentley, Mary Smith looked back and remembered. She remembered the boring relationship she had endured those 20 years ago with Richard Milton.

He had become another piece of minimalist furniture in her penthouse. That had happened just after she had established her publishing company and they definitely had irreconcilable differences. They either fought against each other endlessly or sat around in an absolute and unbearable silence.

Their sex had also proved tedious and Mary Smith came to hate the way that blonde eyebrow always arched when Richard's orgasm shot. She also despised the way he never bothered to show any enthusiasm. She never saw a drop of sweat bead under that thick line of blond hair.

To sum up, he never made any effort, maybe was because of his arrogance, bloody hell, and his damned, disgusting cynicism and superiority.

"Fuck you Richard Milton!"

14
Bleakness

Monday, 6th January 2014

A week after the Marcus and Andreu's fight the classes started once again. Everything seemed to be going from strength to strength. On top of that, Andreu's heart was excited to see that - for the first time since his arrival in Los Angeles - Fernanda had finally plucked up the courage to contact him. Fernanda's email apologized for not responding to any of his previous mails. She said this was due only to a lack of courage on her behalf.

"I know it's been a while without me explaining to you what is going on here, but my heart was confused by our last unfinished conversation. I need you to know that I had to repress my feelings towards you and while I have been dying to hear from you, I'm afraid it's not a personal matter that has driven me to send you this message. It was over a year ago that your mother made me promise to never tell you this, but the situation is now untenable and I think it's better that you know. Do you remember the day you received the news that you could travel abroad to fulfill your dream of becoming a baseball player or a great doctor? The only thing that stopped you was that you had no money to cover your expenses, but your mother didn't want you not to follow your dream. For months she tried to get Nestlé to lend her the money, but time and time again her request was rejected. She knew that no bank would lend her the money either so she was forced to sign a contract with Mr. Priscillian and with his high interest rates too. She placed your home as a guarantee in case she couldn't pay off the borrowed money. I am telling you this because I just don't know what to do. You know that your mother and I would sell our souls to help you fulfill your dreams, but now time has caught up with us and I am afraid that you and your family are about to lose your home because we can't pay back the money to Mr. Priscillian. All of your friends have done everything that they can possibly do, but the debt is too large, and the truth is that now we are running out of ideas. I know that the only person who is left to help us is you.

Forever yours
Fernanda

With a heavy feeling pressing down on his chest, Andreu ran to the campus fields in search of fresh air. Following the fight with Marcus he thought that all his troubles were over, but since receiving Fernanda's message about his mother's secret and the situation back at home his world seemed to be collapsing inwards again.

"There will be a time to think about how to solve these things." He said to himself. "For now I have to concentrate on tomorrow's game. It is possible that this could be the lifeline that we both need at the moment."

15

The Paparazzi (part two)

That same day, January 6, 2014, in New York Mary Smith was overjoyed. She had finally got back to work after what she considered to be a long holiday period.

After her morning exercises and breakfast, she chose a green suit because it is said that green is the color of hope, and it was therefore the right color for the New Year.

Sitting on her swivel chair she could not help but look back on the meeting she had had with her second former husband, Thomas Davis, in Masa, the Japanese restaurant at 12:30.

"You know I still love you." Tom had whispered while savoring the delicate aroma of his sushi.
"How could you lie to me, Tom?" Mary scolded him tenderly. "You knew I wanted to have children."
"We could have adopted." He bowed his head as he replied in his characteristic dreamy romantic tone. Tom didn't seem to belong in the present he was more like an 18th century romantic poet.
"But you lied to me." She said with disdain.

"You know what your problem is." Tom replied. "You are so practical and a hundred thousand times more reasonable and perfect than others. And that is your problem, for all your perfection, you forget how to live."

Tom stood up and without saying another word; Tom stalked out of the restaurant without caring about the paparazzi and their photos. Mary Smith was left alone in Masa thinking that maybe this man was the one who really continued to love her.

****

Margaret knocked on the office door, waking Mary from her memories.

"Come in." Mary answered while catching site of the window cleaners on the scaffolding outside her office window. Their rippling muscles beautiful even beneath the layers of clothing worn to protect them from the bitter cold outside.
"Good morning Miss." Margaret said with a smile.
"Good morning Margaret." Mary replied coldly.

The two women paused to admire the window cleaners stretching and bending outside.

"I wish it was summer so we could see them stripped to the waist again." Mary commented as she cleared her throat and secretly pinched her thigh.

"Of yes." Margaret corroborated with an enthusiastic sigh.

16
The Paparazzi (part three)

Simon Onfray, Mary Smith's third former husband, had deep tanned skin from years of exposure to the sun. He enjoyed vacations in Europe, where he would jump from bed to bed; from blonde to brunette or redhead since Simon did not discriminate in love, he only cared for satisfying his lusts.

The cut of his brown hair, with the fringe that flopped over eyes gave him the air of the American-French intellectual. His taste for elegant scarves, hats and gloves accentuated his artistic style even more. It was therefore no surprise to discover that Simon was a painter.

On 1st January they met for dinner at Alain Ducasse, a restaurant that charged a thousand dollars for its fine

American sourced food that was cooked with French style and flair.

Mary Smith arrived at precisely half past six and joined Simon in the sophisticated atmosphere that very much accommodated his refined tastes.

"You look as beautiful as always." Simon said as he devoured Mary with his eyes. "You have always been so elegant and so perfect, my dear Mary."

Simon's compliments made Mary feet nauseous. She closed her eyes and took a few deep breaths to regain her composure before opening them wide once more.

"And if you always found me so beautiful Simon, why did I find you with another woman in my bed? Fuck you Simon, our marriage didn't even last a month."
"It was just a slip." He answered with a sheepish look.
"A slip? Damn you Simon."

Ever controlled Mary took her seat and quietly calmed herself down before examining her former partner with curiosity.

"You were always so ... so severe." Simon continued. "Breakfast at this hour, always eat lunch at this other time and then make love on these days of the week and at this hour." Simon shook his head. "I couldn't stand it, Mary. I couldn't put up with your regulations and perfection."

Mary bristled with indignation at Simon's expressionless face.

'Not a single month ... we didn't even last for not one month ... You were unfaithful immediately. Why didn't you give me a chance? Why didn't you tell me all this then?"

The silent pause was broken by a storm of paparazzi erupting into the restaurant and snapping Mary and Simon. It took the waiter five minutes to contain them and hurry them to the exit.

"It would have never worked out, Mary." Simon said smiling weakly. "You'll never change."

As she finished her desert Mary bit back on a reply, but the steady gaze of her crystal eyes were fixed upon Simon spoke volumes about what she really felt.

"We'll see my dear." She whispered as she rose from her seat. "We'll see if I ever change. Life is full of pleasant surprises, my friend. One day you will be surprised." Mary concluded as she turned and walked towards the exit.

As she reached the door, Simon shouted: "I hope so my dear Mary." Then he leapt from his seat and ran towards her. Taking her by the arm he whispered into her ear: "Life is too short, my beautiful princess, don't waste it away."

17

Trojans versus Stamford

Tuesday, 7th January 2014

This would be the biggest game of his promising career so far. Around noon, the two teams charged out onto the field: the Trojans and Stamford.

The first three entries were dominated by the powerful batting of the visitors, who won by a margin of six runs to three. It was at that moment that Robert sent Andreu out as the new relay.

In the box, Andreu launched again and again as Robert gave instructions of how to control the game. Soon it was the turn of the Trojans to defend, but it was the arm of Andreu that commanded the game. Throughout the following two entries he managed to control the adversary attack, no one could connect to Andreu's fastball or elliptical curves.

Although the score remained down by one run, something began eating at the promising newcomer. His right arm was beginning to bother him from the elbow down; perhaps it was not yet fully recovered from the fight with Marcus the week before.

"Come on, demonic arm, you must resist." He said to himself over and over again. "I didn't think Marcus' face was that hard."

And a slight smile formed on Andreu's lips. The warm memory helped to encourage him to forget the pain.

Then the ball slipped through his fingers without enough power, which let the batter give it a good strike. At this point Robert beckoned Andreu to come in for a chat.

"What is it boy? That batter was easy to control and you let it go." Robert demanded.
"I don't feel good coach. My elbow is killing me."
"Listen well to what I say. You can't lose this match, there is too much at stake for you." Robert admonished him. "So you go back out there and show everyone the kind of stuff you're made of. If you want some extra motivation think of your family back in Cuba, hoping for you to become a famous player."

Andreu's thoughts went back to remember Fernanda's message. A fierce brightness suddenly burned his eyes.

"Robert, you're right. I have to do this for my family."

Back out on the field Andreu's performance improved and the game ended in a Trojans victory even if only by a minimum difference. Andreu's pain was gone, overtaken by the motivation of helping his family.

"I have to recover my mother's home at any cost."

As Andreu remembered Fernanda's final phrase: forever yours, a sore loser from Stamford pitched the ball at Andreu's head. Those few seconds took the edge off his concentration and Andreu did not see that the ball streaking towards him at 100 miles per hour. The blow was brutal – hitting him in the right parietal knocking him to the ground.

****

It was two hours before Andreu regained consciousness.

"Where am I? What happened?" He asked heatedly. "You received a hard knock on the head." The doctor explained patiently. "We've taken some x-rays and have ruled out a possible fracture, but until we get the results of the MRI we can't discharge you. This is for your own safety since there may be the possibility of an internal injury to the brain. Try to rest, it will help you recover faster."

At that the doctor left.

18

Happy New York

It was January 14th 2014 when Andreu was discharged from hospital and returned to his room on campus. On arrival he was delighted to meet Johan who had some news for his dear friend.

"I see that you did not die Cuban shit." Johan said by way of a greeting.
"Not before you do gringo crap." Andreu replied, as they merged into a fraternal embrace.

"But tell me what are you doing here, Johan? You said you were going to be at your mother's house and that you were very excited because your grandparents were coming to visit and you hadn't seen for a long time."
"I decided to stay. I could not leave without saying goodbye. I went to see my father instead and I stayed

with him for a few days. Now I have something very important to tell you."

"But you hate your father Johan. What made you change your mind?" Andreu asked his curiosity piqued.

"Let's just say it was the Christmas spirit that made me rethink my relationship with my old chap." Johan shrugged.

"Well tell me what this important thing is that you have to say?" Andreu enquired.

Johan said no more and simply handed over a letter signed by Robert and by the Sports Council of the University of Southern Califronia:

Dear Andreu:

We regret to inform you that after your injury, we must rescind your invitation to play in the big leagues.

We appreciate your commitment and hard work, which we have found commendable. However, due to your injury, we do not believe that you are fit enough for the big league and therefore our contract with you is now closed.

We wish you all the luck with your future and we take this opportunity to send a cordial greeting.

Andreu looked uninterested but sad.

"Well, nothing happens Johan." Andreu said pausing to scratch his chin. "This is just another bump in the road. Next year will be different, you'll see. Also if I don't become a professional player I will always have my medicine, which is my other passion."
"But that's not all of it Andreu." Johan interrupted. "The fight you had with Marcus was uploaded to the Internet and reached the ears of Dean Johnson and he has asked the board to have your scholarship withdrawn. Now your fees will have to be paid out of your pocket if you want to continue with your studies here." Johan said as he handed him another letter.

Johan found it difficult to find anything to say while Andreu read the second letter, he felt both angry and helpless.

"But I have talked to my father. "Johan finally continued with difficulty. "He told me that you could live in our apartment in New York free of charge and he has also contacted an old friend, one Richard Milton, who has certain connections and if you want he can get a job in the publishing or editorial company of his ex-wife. There is nothing else I can do." He concluded.

"Do not worry my dear friend." Andreu replied with a shake of his head. "You've done more than enough. But if I go, I will take Marcus between the legs." He added in a mumble.

Once again - in a fit of rage - Andreu left the house in search of his attacker. He crossed the field leading to the house of Sigma Alpha Epsilon, but a sudden thought stopped him in his tracks. Marcus was no longer on campus and what could he get by repeating the beating anyway? He turned and gently paced back to his own room.

Johan was still there making the final preparations for his departure.

"Is the offer still on? Andreu asked with regained composure.

Johan smiled and handed over the keys to the New York apartment.

At this stage of our "plot", Andreu could not imagine the complicated skeins of life tied with tangled knots and obscured by blurred pasts that bedevil our existence.

****

"Richard." The tremulous female voice murmured edged with mitigated pain.
"Is that you?" Exclaimed Richard eager to drink in her words. "Tell me, my love."
"I have always kept the card you gave me with your name and phone number, even though I never thought that I would need it." She took a deep breath. "But I need your help now."
"Any time." Richard sighed. "I hope you will forgive me someday."
"You're forgiven. You never did anything wrong. But please, help me." She earnestly begged.
"I surely will." Richard confirmed as tears welled up in his eyes.

Two days later. 16th January 2014

An iconic New York Yellow Cab pulled up at the address that Johan had provided Andreu in the Big Apple.

Andreu was taken aback when he entered the luxurious apartment. Without being an expert anyone could appreciate the refined taste of Johan's family. The view from the heights was impressive: down below was Central Park in all its glory - and lower Manhattan. In short, everything Andreu had heard about from the most glamorous city in the United States was now laid out before his eyes.

He unfolded Johan's note with the instructions he was to follow:

"9:30 A.M. Monday 20 January, meeting with Margaret, "Editorial Miss MS".

And a final sentence:

"Be punctual please. Do not blow it this time".
Johan

19
The world of connections

On Friday January 10, 2014, Mary Smith was seated in her office reading through the first chapters of the latest novel submitted by Orlando The Great, *Mexican Love*, when Margaret timidly knocked at her door.

"Come in." Mary instructed brusquely.
"Good morning ma'am. Sorry to interrupt you, but your former first husband, Richard Milton is waiting for you outside and he says he needs to see you."

Surprised, Mary did not answer at first. A beam of light broke through the clouds outside and focused on Mary's face. For that moment Margaret thought that her boss with that radiant light looked like a graven image of a goddess with that rock hard expression, imperious gaze and the arrogant pose of that haughty body. The light from outside was playing games with Mary's countenance; her skin looked like a piece of pure silk the lines of her face showing in its solemn folds.

"Richard" She replied, and the instinctive affection after knowing him for twenty long years showed through. "That's weird. Tell him to come right in."

Margaret spun around, rushed towards the door and beckoned Richard in. He shrugged off his Burberry raincoat and handed it to Margaret together with his hat and Aquascutum scarf, revealing the elegantly tailored Savile Row below and flashed Mary his signature eyebrow arch.

"Richard." Mary said with a hint of sarcasm. "I thought we had already seen each other for this year."
"I come to ask you for a favor." Richard replied coldly, but inside he was burning, as it was very important for him to keep the promise he had made twenty-five years ago to that tremulous voice. "You know this is the first time in twenty years that I am going to ask you for anything."
"OK." Mary said and gestured to him to take a seat, "I'm all ears."

Unable to find an excuse to linger and listen further Margaret closed the door behind her and left them alone together.

"I hope this isn't one of your tasteless jokes." Mary stated with a wry smile.

"No it's not a joke." Richard pronounced calmly, his face contracting into a grim expression. Richard was a man of his word and 25 years ago he had made a promise.

"Tell me then." She said as a mocking silent laughter swelled behind her lips.

"I have a friend whose son, Johan is studying at the University of Southern California." Richard began to explain and Mary was intrigued by where this story was likely to go. "And Johan has a friend who Johan is a Cuban, I believe his name is Andreu, who is now out of a scholarship after being dropped from the University baseball team."

"I See." Mary leaned forward as she interrupted. "Can you cut the story short, get straight to the point and tell me just what you want me to do?"

"Offer the Cuban a job in your publishing house, Miss perfect Mary Smith." Richard replied with a touch of irritation.

"All right my dear. I will but you're still so fucking unbearable." She exclaimed flashing Richard a vague wide eyed smile.

"Thank you dear." Richard replied with an arch of both eyebrows.

'Are his papers all in order?" Mary asked enjoying Richard's humiliation at having to ask her for a favor.

"Yes. He has an indefinite leave to stay in the United States. I was the one who took arranged that." Richard answered his chest swelling with pride.

"All right Richard. Let's do this. Go and explain all this to Margaret and she will arrange an interview for the boy and sort out everything else. Is that okay my dear?" She concluded with an air of elegant detachment.

"I think that's just great, honey." He riposted sarcastically, having had quite enough of Mary's intolerable treatment, He didn't like being talked to like a servant.

"Anything else my dear?" She added thinking back to the domestic quarrels they had endured for that long seeming year and ten days twenty years ago.

"Nothing else, my dear." Richard replied as he rose from his seat. Mary maliciously placed her elbow on the table to rest her cheek in her right hand as if to say that she had already given Richard her full attention and now it was time for him to leave.

****

Once Richard had left, Mary buzzed Margaret and asked her to come back into her office.

"Yes Miss Smith?" Margaret acknowledged Mary with a concerned tone.

"Have you spoken to Richard?" Mary asked. Margaret frowned and nodded. "I guess you have arranged everything by now."

"Yes Miss Smith. I have arranged the interview for a Mr. Andreu Santa Rosa. He will be with me on Monday, January 20th at 9:30 AM. But…" Margaret paused suddenly.

"What is it?" Mary enquired harshly.

Put on the spot Margaret resolutely forced herself to speak.

"Well what kind of job should I offer the Cuban? I think he is only 23 or 24 years old and he was training to be a doctor before he was thrown out of the university."

Margaret relaxed and took in a deep breath. For the first time in her life she had spoken up for herself in front of Mary Smith.

"I have no idea." Mary exclaimed with a knowing grin, she liked this new more determined Margaret. "No matter what he says in the interview, you are going to employ him anyway."

"But doing what?" She bristled again and earned a smirk in return from Mary. Oh yes, she liked this new Margaret very much.

"How many years of medical training has he done?" Mary asked as she placed an index finger on each temple.

"Four years I believe." Margaret muttered.

"Well, in this country if someone has done four years of medicine, they can perfectly well work in first aid or as a nurse or even a head nurse, right?" Mary explained and Margaret's eyes were filled with admiration for Mary's creative problem solving.

"It's a wonderful idea, ma'am."

"We have fourteen floors. Assign a medical room for him on every floor and remember whatever he says in the interview, even if he completely fuck it up, give him the job."

"Very well Miss Smith."

20
The interview

At 7:50 AM on Monday, January 20 Andreu's alarm went off with a maddening and impertinent melody. This was rewarded with a loud slap. Andreu stretched out his limbs. Every one of his numb muscles felt as if it was trying to burst through his skin.

It was a normal Monday for most people in the Big Apple, but not for Andreu, having recently arrived from California he was finding it difficult to adapt to hustle and bustle of the New York lifestyle.

Andreu stepped into the bathroom to wash his athletic body. He liked to shower in cold water, according to a medical article he had read this helped to encourage the circulation of the blood, but he had actually began his cold shower habit when a beautiful blond lady tourist with a penchant for photography, had advised him to do so while she snapped some pictures of him for her journal.
He still remembered the words of the beautiful foreign woman.

"Nothing arouses my senses faster in the morning than the contrast of the cold water cascading down your burning body."

Andreu spent ten minutes having his skin invigorated by the shower, and then he put on his very best clothes – every item freshly laundered and pressed. He didn't have anything showy or with designer labels, but what he was wearing made him look pretty good. He exited the building and headed towards the address Johan had given him. On the same note was scribbled the name John, Johan's father, to remind him just in case anybody asked who had recommended him.

At the kerb he hesitated, should he take a taxi? Trouble was the money in his pockets was limited and he could not really afford such luxuries, but on the other hand he didn't want to get lost either On the street corner he noticed a hot dog stall. "Who better than a hot dog seller to direct a clueless person like me?" Andreu thought. The hot dogs and the frying onions smelt delicious, and Andreu could not resist the temptation to sample one, although the last thing he needed was a blob of hot dog grease on his interview clothes "The Miss MS Publishing House is right over there" the hot dog vendor pointed towards a towering edifice above the treetops of Central Park. "You can't miss it, it's that great big pink building over there. You have to cut around the circuit of Central Park and it is approximately three miles from here." The hot dog vendor explained. "Where are you from?"
"I'm Cuban. Thanks for the information." Andreu answered. He quickly checked his clothes for hot dog

crumbs and grease before setting off for the big pink tower

"Hey." The hot dog vendor called out to him with a sparkle in his naughty eyes. "Are you gonna come back to my stall sometime?"

"Sure friend." Andreu howled back from the distance. "I like your hot dogs." Andreu laughed and waved the vendor goodbye.

He checked the hands on his watch and it was now 9:15 AM; he only had fifteen minutes left to make it on time for his interview, so he decided to run the circuit of Central Park until he reached his destination. It was 9:36 when the doorman opened up the ornately decorated glass doors at the entrance to Miss MS Publishing. Inside the words "Miss MS" were everywhere he looked. He paused just for a moment in the foyer as he tried recovering both his breath and his composure.

****

Time and time again Andreu checked the time on his watch. He unfolded Johan's note once more: "please be punctual, do not blow it this time ". Those words hurried him on his way to the reception desk, where a mature uniformed woman was examining some papers while talking into a telephone headset simultaneously.

"Good Morning. Could you tell me where the office of Mrs. Margaret is?" Andreu asked said with an innocent smile. "I have an appointment for a job interview with her at 9:30 this morning."
"You mean MISS Margaret? I presume." The receptionist haughtily replied.
"Mrs. or Miss? Who cares if she sleeps alone or with someone?" Andreu petulantly shrugged. "Please Just show me where I have to go." He added impatiently.
"Look just in case you haven't noticed these are the offices of Miss MS: the largest and most profitable publisher not only in the USA, but in the world; and the least you can do is show some respect, especially if you are looking to be hired in a place like this."
"OK I thank you infinitely for your semantic class, but now, would you be so kind as to tell me where MISS Margaret's office is, please?" Andreu enquired with a special emphasis on the word MISS.
"Go down the hall on the left, turn left again and you will find yourself in the elevator lobby, then take the elevator up to level 14. Take the hall is on the right and you will find a door with her name. MISS Margaret has

two offices: one on the fourteenth floor and another one on the first floor."

"Thanks". Andreu responded without really having understood the directions and why a second office was mentioned. "That was all I needed." He added sarcastically.

"But ... " The receptionist interrupted. "You said you had a job interview with Miss Margaret?"

"Ándale. That's what I told you that from the very beginning." Andreu complained taking a nervous look at his watch. It was already 9:42 AM.

"Name please? The stony faced receptionist.

"I am in a state of shock.'" Andreu muttered through his clenched teeth. "My name is Andreu Santa Rosa."

"Then you do not have to go up to the office on the 14th floor." She replied.

"Well you could have told me that in the first place." He replied crossing his arms.

"Had you explained properly from the very beginning, we would not have wasted so much time and I could have told you that the interview you have booked with Miss Margaret at 9:30am is not in her office on the 14th floor."

"I think I am going to have a fit, Madame receptionist." Andreu complained while she giggled at his discomfort.

"Your interview is in the boardroom, which is at the end of the hallway behind you." The receptionist could not help sniggering.

"But you just told me it was on the 14th floor and then..."

"Now just hang on a moment." She interrupted him, becoming serious once more. "You asked for the Miss Margaret's office, but she is not in her office right now. Oh no, she is waiting for you in the boardroom. Now do you understand the importance of telling me exactly why you are here young man?"

Andreu turned his back on her without further acknowledgement, knowing that if he engaged any further with that woman he would eventually be driven to explode.

"I'd hurry if I were you. Miss Margaret hates people being late, clock is ticking and it is now 9: 50."

In the corridor an intellectual looking young woman in a pair of Jimmy Choo spectacles gave Andreu directions to the boardroom. Passing through another reception area, which was thankfully unmanned at this hour, Andreu plucked up the courage to knock at the door a couple of times. There was no response, so he took the initiative to enter uninvited. Inside he found a large executive table surrounded by a dozen executive chairs, but no Miss Margaret. Feeling defeated, he took a seat.

"Damn, but what have I done? Here time is like water." "He muttered to himself as he looked at his watch for a third time, and observed little hand marking the number 10." I have let down Johan and all thanks to that crazy receptionist bitch, who messed me around while knowing all the time I would be late for my interview. "

At that very moment a well dressed woman entered the boardroom. Andreu feeling defeated spun listlessly around in his appropriated chair.

"Excuse me, are you Mr. Andreu Santa Rosa?" The woman asked him and he morosely nodded. "Hello, I am Mary Smith's personal secretary and right hand person. My name is Margaret." Andreu felt a chill run down his spine. "I apologize for my delay. Have you been waiting for long?"
"Okay." Andreu replied with a nervous smile. "Just as well this is publishing as a delay like this in a hospital could mean the difference between life and death! Andreu joked.

"I beg your pardon, what did you just say?" Margaret said in a tone reminiscent of Miss Mary Smith. After so many years working for her boss, Margaret was becoming more and more like her. She extended her hand and passed him some documents.
"I'm Sorry, I didn't mean to offend." He snorted and gave her his CV.

Margaret had heard Andreu's comment and had to cover her mouth while pretending that she was reading his CV, so that Andreu could not see that she was secretly amused.

"Please read the documents I have just given you and when you have the time sign the contract. Now ... " Margaret paused. "I must make this crystal clear to you Mr. Santa Rosa. You are here for only one reason: you have been recommended. I'm going to be watching you like a hawk, so make sure that you do an exemplary job. Have you understood everything I said?"
"Perfectly well and I can assure you that you will not regret it. And if you allow me a question Miss Margaret, what exactly am I going to be doing here?"
"All Right. We already knew about your four years of medical school. That's why Mrs. Smith has decided to set you up with a medical room, for which you will be

entirely responsible. It will be located on the sixth floor and you will start working here full time from Monday 27 January. You have the rest of this week to rest and acclimatize to New York. Any doubts Mr. Santa Rosa?"
"No doubts, but please delete the Mister, just call me Andreu."
"Any doubts Andreu?"
"No." the Cuban responded.
"Well Andreu, welcome to MissMS and I trust our faith in you will not be misplaced?"

They shook hands.

"One more thing Andreu. Even though you have the rest of this week off before you come back to work here on Monday, this week you will need to introduce yourself to Miss. Smith. You must meet with her and tell her who you are so that she knows your face. Miss Mary Smith likes to meet each and every one of the employees who work for her personally."
"No problem." Said Andreu. "When can I do that?"
"She's always very busy, but the best day for you to meet her is this Thursday at her office at quarter past twelve sharp."

21
The Shoe

Thursday January 23, 2014

Andreu was hurrying from the ground floor of the building to the first, with a nasty knot beginning to form in his throat. "Where the hell was the damn office of Mary Smith?" Margaret had made an appointment to meet the boss on Thursday at 12.15. It should have been a very simple matter, but with all this running around from one place to another, he no longer knew where he was. He blamed the sarcastic receptionist who, just like the last time he visited the building, had confused him with all her convoluted explanations. First she had told him with a wry smile that Mary Smith's office was on the 14th floor, then on the first floor and finally with a sarcastic laugh she explained that Mrs. Smith had a private office in each of the building's fourteen floors and at that very moment she would be in her office on the first floor.

'Well, you could have told me that in the beginning, I am so lucky that I seem to have met a joker of a receptionist." Andreu thought to himself.

He gazed at the plaque on the wall in the hallway and saw the number one. So he was definitely on the right floor. Now he just had to locate the office that belonged to the big boss. "Damn, where is her office?"

Desperate not to be late, Andreu sped down the corridor where as he tried to keep track of the names printed on the doors, he collided with a delicate female figure.

"I am so sorry, so very sorry." Andreu stuttered. "Oh my god, what a thick ear I have given you, I'm so sorry!"

The woman struggled to her knees, as if she was in a position of supplication before him. Obviously embarrassed she attempted to straighten her skirt, which had risen to expose her underwear in the fall. Andreu took the initiative, bent down and lifted her up by her waist. The woman, still in an evident state of confusion, allowed herself to be held in his strong embrace for longer than would seem necessary.

"I am really sorry ma'am. Are you alright?"

She said nothing.

"Mamma mia. You even lost your shoe." Andreu quickly ducked down and retrieved the delicate shoe and with a touch of enthusiastic gallantry he attempted to replace the shoe on the lady's foot. "I can never understand how women are able to walk in these things." He added nervously. "It must be like juggling when you walk. You have very pretty ankles by the way."

Mary Smith roared with laughter.

"Well at least you seem to have cheered up." Andreu smiled and as his words escaped his lips their warmth gently caressed the cold cheeks of Mary Smith. "My name Andreu. Andreu Santa Rosa." He introduced himself while she fixed her crystal blue eyes onto his black shining gaze.

At that moment when Mary Smith and Andreu stared into each other's eyes, their irises connected and she experienced those penetrating green eyes for the very first time, and noted how the whites were free of any stains. Those were the playful and affectionate eyes of a sorcerer.

"I'm sorry I don't know your name?" He asked her unable to turn away from her celestial blue, but mischievous eyes.

"My name is Mary." She replied as she placed one hand upon his shoulder while she adjusted the fit of her shoe.

The touch of her hand on his shoulder unleashed an intimate and strange feeling of warmth that spread throughout both their bodies.

"Mary what?" Andreu innocently enquired while inhaling her languid musky perfume.

"Just Mary." She replied.

Her hand was still on his shoulder, while he still rested his on her shapely hips. Both seemed frozen at the spot as an electric shiver ran through their suddenly defenseless bodies.

"You seem to be lost." She broke the silence and pinched her right thigh hard in an effort to regain control of her feelings. A drop of blood slid smoothly down her thigh towards her knee.

"Yes." He replied trying to shake himself back to a semblance of normality. "I am looking for the boss's office, you know Miss. Mary Smith."

"Very well then." She said as she extricated herself from his grip and turned away from him. "It's right here. Follow me please."

"Thanks." Andreu sighed as he ran his eyes over her shapely back.

PART TWO: INTERMISSION

In our evolutionary processes - in the ways of our lives –
we, humans suffer from "little intermissions".

22
Heavy Psychic Whisper

Thursday, 23rd January at 12:15 PM

As Andreu followed Mary Smith down the corridor, a voice in his head repeated the same phrase over and over to him: "What the hell is happening to me? What the hell is happening to me" The memory of the brief touch of that narrow waist, her shapely hips and the deep musky smell of her perfume was making him blush like a schoolboy even though she was at least 20 years older than him. Now following right behind her as she led him down that long corridor, he could enjoy without any hindrance the rear view and without any doubt he appreciated it. She was quite stunning. He could not understand his weakness, that unusual and uncontrollable sexual that she aroused in him.

The heels of Mary Smith's Laboutins clicked along the polished marble of the corridor. She could feel Andreu's appreciative gaze boring into her back, making her feel like a "swinging pendulum" and she was having trouble controlling those trembling legs. The single droplet of blood expressed by that vicious pinch continued to run slowly down her leg until it reached her right foot. She placed both hands on her temples trying to work out her confused her emotions. Her sensual arousal was making her feel on edge. She had never experienced such a powerful attraction towards any man, such unbridled sensuality.

"Come on, follow me in please." She indicated with her trembling hand towards the highly polished black door of her office, a black so deep as if it was an invitation to her dark and sterile internal world.

Clearly imprinted on the door, in gold blocked letter was the name: Mary Smith.

"Thank you." He said and his dark eyes glittered as he took in the room's interior.
"Do come in and take a seat please." She said indicating a chair in front of the antique desk with her eyes.

Andreu sat where he had bid and watched as the mysterious woman walked the desk and sat right opposite him on the swivel chair. Twice Andreu attempted to open up a conversation with her and twice he couldn't find the words, so finally he shrugged his shoulders and stated:

"I've come here to introduce myself to Mary Smith. " He experienced feeling a dark foreboding.

Mary Smith leaned forward and said quietly with her characteristic coldness:

"I am Mary Smith."

Both remained silent. Andreu felt a very nasty lump rising into his throat and at that moment he hated himself for the impetuosity and strength of his youth. However, despite his discomfort, this woman, who was going to be his boss, still inexplicably excited him. "Andreu, you're once again into deep trouble." He said to himself.

Mary Smith though was overwrought; under the desk she pinched her thigh once again while her coldly organized mind attempted to find logical explanations for the way she felt. "There is no dignity in my illogical arousal." She kept repeating to herself. "The more I think about this subject, the less I understand."

Andreu nervously attempted to open the conversation once again "I do not know if you agree with me Miss. Smith, but I think that I have made quite a mess this time."

A dry laugh escaped from Mary Smith's lips in an effort to clear her throat and hopefully dismiss the whole incident.

"I propose that we should forget everything that has just happened and start again.' She rejoined, secretly admiring that pagan love that prohibited sexuality.

Andreu nodded, but still could not understand his feelings. He thought he should only be excited by the pretty young girls, with the fresh and juicy meat and yet now that mature woman was awakening his animal lusts from within.

"Tell me then why you have come here." Mary said taking in the features of the young man sat before her. His cherry lips seemed to be like the two halves of a fruit.
"Margaret asked me to come and introduce myself to you." Andreu stated through those juicy lips displaying the pearl white teeth hidden behind them.
"Okay. I hope you will enjoy your new job here."
"I certainly will do. I also hope you will be satisfied with my work." Andreu replied trying to hide the

mischievous signs of arousal that his body was unconsciously giving away.

"All Right. Well goodbye Andreu, it was nice to meet you." Mary Smith dropped her eyes to check the documents on her desk.

"Goodbye Miss Smith." He said as he rose from his seat and Mary could not help but admire his superbly developed pectorals and biceps through the translucently thin fabric of his white shirt.

She left the papers, stood up and walked around her desk. Standing in front of him once more they attempted to shake hands professionally, but both of them felt the flesh of their hands burn. Andreu lowered his gaze to her feet, while she looked up towards the ceiling.

With his head down, he noticed the trails of blood droplets running g down her right thigh, past her knee towards her foot.

"You appear to be bleeding, Miss. Smith." He said and Mary collapsed into the seat he had just vacated. "Let me take a look at that." Mary Smith was powerless to resist. Silently he lifted her skirt to reveal the deep wound in her thigh, clearly the result of self-harm. "But why do you hurt yourself?" He shook his head as he asked her.

"Please just leave me alone Andreu." She asked as he shook his head in disbelief, trying to understand how that labyrinthine tortured soul in front of him was capable of abusing her own thigh until it bled.
"I do not understand." He stated sadly. "Why do you hurt yourself?"

Recovering her composure Mary Smith could see that Andreu was going to be persistent. She got up quickly, turned and walked away from him towards the panoramic window. "Why the hell had she done that favor for her ex, Richard Milton?"

"Goodbye Andreu." Mary Smith uttered with finality, having seemingly regained her composure like a phoenix rising from her own ashes.
"Goodbye Madame." Andreu turned around and loped out of the office, slamming the door as he went.

Mary Smith screamed in fury. Damn. Nobody, absolutely nobody, had ever slammed a door on her.

23
A whimsical twist of fate

His orders were clear. Andreu was to arrive punctually on 27th January at nine o'clock for his first day at work. By then a complete medical room had been prepared for him on the first floor just above the printing press on the ground floor. Miss Mary Smith was an excellent businesswoman with her financially astute mind, so she wanted to get the most out of Andreu. On the one hand she was doing her former husband a favor, but on the other - with the excuse - she and her company would benefit from having Andreu around. Since the American medical system is very expensive, Mary Smith thought about killing two birds with one stone. On the one hand, by locating the clinic close to the manufacturing floors she would offer better protection to her employees since more accidents were likely to happen in the industrial zone where the books were printed and finished, than on the floors occupied by departments like marketing and human resources; but on the other hand, as well as creating a safer working environment Mary Smith was also putting into place an innovative and revolutionary idea in the United States of America. She could already visualize the headlines on the covers of the magazines and newspapers: Mary Smith, the famous business woman, the richest woman in USA has established a new model for American companies, one which provides its employees with free workplace medical care.

She was pleased to have found, once again, another means to generating positive media coverage for her company, but over that weekend, she had trouble concentrating on anything. The image of young Andreu kept coming into her mind.

It was that accidental collision, that whimsical twist of fate that had thrown her mind into confusion. Daydreaming about the Cuban had been a crazy affair for the whole weekend she reflected and shrugged in resignation.

"Good." She said to herself with a sigh. "I'll talk to him first thing Monday morning when he starts his first day at work. I must stop this ASAP." She scolded herself on Friday evening.

But it just kept haunting her through Saturday and then on through Sunday. Mary found that she could not control the trembling in her legs and the confused sensuous visions exploding in her head.

She had slept badly over the whole weekend and when she woke up on Monday morning she was in a foul mood. "Oh yes, I will have to talk to Andreu ASAP."

Andreu woke up on Monday morning with a wicked smile wrapped around his face. It was as if his lips were dusted with an accumulation of flavors. Night after night since he had met Mary Smith he had fantasized again and again about drawing imaginary maps on her body, on the warmth of her mouth and on the heat of her sex.

Just visualizing her naked body in his imagination brought on a rock hard erection: the idea of his avid tongue tickling her pink nipples, making them wet with his saliva and the warmth of his breath making them harden in his lips. The notion of violently tearing open her blouse, ripping off each and every one of the pearly buttons, while cornering up her against the wall, placing his mouth over hers, the very idea was so much more exciting, teasing, arousing.

Andreu could see himself as the weakest half of the partnership, because of his impulsive need to kiss her frantically but he could not help it. He dreamed of having her naked in the bed next to him, panting and perspiring in the afterglow of their lovemaking.

Four nights had gone by since he had first met her. In his dreams he first kissed the corner of her lips, there where only a few know just how wonderful it feels; then gently moving on to kiss her cheeks, but only for a few seconds, then breathing out and whispering into her ear that 'tonight would be the night.'

"You'll be mine, Miss. Smith. Oh yes one day you will be mine. You will sigh when you feel my sharp teeth gently bite at your ears, and with an explosive desire, you will make me rub my manhood against your bleeding thigh while my lustful fingers will caress the margins of your sex

24

Andreu's medical room

Indeed, by Monday 27th January 2014, Andreu's dispensary was perfectly prepared with everything in its place, located on the first floor of the buildings industrial heart.

Mary Smith was still sulking. All weekend she had been thinking about that Cuban who had the nerve to slam her office door. Who did he think he was? No one had ever slammed a door on her like that. In a momentary fit of anger, she thought of bursting into his medical room and telling him a couple of things, but instead she stepped back and mused: "It will be better to leave things the way they are."

Monday 27 went by, Tuesday 28 and Wednesday 29 followed and Andreu took every opportunity when he was not covering his duty at the dispensary to sneak out onto the first floor to where Mary Smith was usually to be found. It would only be for a few seconds, but if his luck held he could sneak a look at her and sometimes even get a nod of recognition back.

But for Andreu this was not enough. His first week had passed by and there had been no clear sign from Mary Smith to allow him to make a bold move. She was always so distant, cold and professional and that was driving the Cuban crazy.

"Just signal me. That's all I need to for me to know that this is not just in my head." He thought to himself.

Since that day when they had first met and he had lifted her skirt and felt her right thigh with the excuse of examining that bleeding wound, Miss. Smith had never again lost her composure in his presence. Every time that look she regaled him with was nothing more than a simple greeting.

But…

Mary Smith, the lady who commanded thousands of men around the world, was struggling to dominate Andreu. He was not commandable, at least not in the ways that she knew and it was against her own instincts not to be in maximum control.

"What has possessed me about that Cuban? Only seeing him is enough to produce a heat throughout my body that lands gently between my legs, and this desire is killing me." She pondered. "How can you be so brutish not to realize that I'm melting? And why am I stupidly falling into your trap without hesitation? "

"But where is my mind?" She wondered quietly. "I could be his mother. He's just a young and immature boy who probably just wants to experience an office adventure."

These last words brought back Mary Smith back to some kind of composure allowing her to return once more to scrutinizing the latest work of Orlando The Great before launching it on to the market.

Two days later, on Friday January 31 Andreu thought of a brilliant excuse to try and get to meet Mary Smith once again.

Using his medical authority, as he had been placed in absolute charge of the health of each and every employee in the Miss MS Company, he asked Margaret to supply him with a complete personnel list. He explained that he wanted to have a complete workplace health control of all of them, in the first place to open a personal medical file for each and everyone of them and secondly so that he could treat them individually according to their needs and medical history.

Unsuspecting, Margaret, who by now was a complete control freak – the absolute projection of Mary Smith - looked favorably on Andreu's purposeful action.

"Thank you Miss Margaret. These documents will be very useful to me." He answered in his sweetest voice. "No, do not thank me Andreu. You have had a wonderful idea. We should have done this a long, long time ago. I told you I was going to be watching you, and your work so far has been extemporary. With this new idea of yours we can contribute to improving the quality of our employees life and also create more good publicity for the company, I shall always be pleased to help you."

Then Margaret said goodbye and briskly walked away. Andreu sat down to review the extensive collection of documents only looking for one name, that of Mary Smith.

"Eureka." Andreu was excited.

Over that weekend Andreu meticulously planned out his strategy. He did not want to start seeing his patients by rank or surname, because that would not help to achieve his goal to force Mrs. Smith to be the last.

Then another brilliant notion lit up his face, although there would be a degree of risk.

"Right. She, being the crown of the company, her position would consequently be the lowest at risk. Miss Smith could not say no to him seeing her for "medical purposes" since, as she was the boss, she was supposed to be a role model and set an example to others.

"I've finally cornered you Mary Smith. This time you can't hide behind your desk." Andreu laughed aloud.

Monday, 3rd February 2014

It was going to be a tough week for Andreu. He worked tirelessly all through it and he even had to take much of the paper work home every night - but that was the least of his concerns - his goal was to reach Friday, February 7, with the intention of seeing, once again the owner of his dreams, and show her everything he had bottled up inside.

Early on Monday February 3, Andreu sent a note to Miss. Smith, via her secretary Margaret. In the note she was requested to attend a medical check up at 4:30 pm on Friday February 7th.

Incandescent with rage Mary Smith demanded from her secretary the meaning of that note.

"It's just a routine examination Miss Smith. All employees will eventually have to have one. You would be the only person who hasn't and that would not do your reputation with the staff any good at all. If you excuse my impertinence I do not see what you are worried about." Margaret concluded tersely.

Completely unaware of her role Margaret, had been the perfect ace in Andreu's hand of cards.

"Excuse me Margaret. I think Mr. Rocamora's breakfast has caused me a little indigestion. That's all for now. Thank you Margaret." Mary dismissed her.

****

Friday February 7th had finally arrived. It had been exactly fourteen days after they had met in the hallway. Fourteen painful days without each other, fourteen seemingly endless days.

It was exactly 4:30 and Andreu was getting anxious to see that the absolute owner of Mary Smith's empire come through the door.

Mary Smith was hesitant to walk along that corridor her medical check up, and again the last words of her secretary echoed in her head: "It can't do you any harm ma'am. It is not a bad idea to have a check up from time to time."

"You have played your cards well Andreu." And a leering smile escaped onto his lips. "I am going to make you fall, Mary Smith, into my own game."

25
Playing with fire

Mary Smith knocked on the surgery door and when she heard the soft, lilting Latino accented "come in", she burst forward into the medical room in just two powerful steps.

"Good afternoon Andreu." Mary greeted him as she closed the door behind her. Her countenance appeared cold, despite her inner feelings.
"Good afternoon ma'am." He replied, fixing his eyes upon her as he rose from his seat. He had forgotten that she was normally as gelid as hard packed snow. "How's your thigh?" He asked with curiosity.
"Never ask me anything else ever again." The icy woman's crystalline cerulean eyes flashed as she gravely replied to him.
"OK. I will not ask you anything else." He took a step forward. "Do sit down please. I need to do an auscultation."
"I don't want you to ask me any more questions." She repeated as Andreu took another step towards her. His blood was boiling. "You are analyzing me. I don't like anybody analyzing me."

Mary Smith could not understand herself. Where had her usual characteristic of cool self-control gone?

'I'm not doing any analyzing." Andreu lied with a disarming shrug. "Please do sit down." Andreu's voice rose to a commanding tone as he uttered the request and she obeyed but not without a note of challenge in those crystalline eyes.

"You know your questions have the power to really irritate me." She exclaimed in resigned exasperation.

"What questions have I asked now?" Andreu replied with a mischievous grin.

Finally Andreu had her sitting on the couch right opposite him. He sat himself down on his stool in front of her and gently opened his legs. Inching himself forward, he gently pressed Mary Smith's legs together with the inside of his thighs.

"Unbutton your shirt please and then take a deep breath." Andreu requested attempting to control his trembling fingers as he placed the stethoscope on her left breast.

"I hate it when you ask me questions." Mary Smith replied, the top of her white shirt now unbuttoned. Her breasts jutted sweet and playful above the brilliant white of her bra.

"Now breathe deeply please." Andreu asked feeling his member enlarging every second. "Now exhale please." His manhood hardened, trapped in that intimate contact between each other's thighs and the sight of her breasts freed from her blouse, accelerated his breathing. "It seems that you have excellent lungs." He said as he removed the stethoscope and enjoyed a long lingering look at her delicate breasts. "What are these questions that I ask that annoy you so much, Miss. Smith?" His manhood was now pressed hard against Mary Smith's hip, surprisingly she found herself adopting a more passive attitude.

"The question you asked me on that first day that we met two weeks ago and the same question you repeated to me today, Andreu, why do I hurt myself. That same question Andreu!" She replied as freed herself from his embrace and leapt up from the coach.

"OK. I will not ask any more questions about it." He sighed sharply. "But will you now let me examine your right thigh please?" Andreu asked as he rose from the stool.

"And I didn't appreciate the way you slammed the door on the way out of my office. How dare you? Who do you think you are?" She cried with fury.

"I won't do it again, I promise." Andreu responded.

"And don't turn your back on me when I'm talking to you." Mary exploded into silent tears. "And I'm not going to let you examine my thigh."

"Why are you crying, Mary?" Andreu asked as he walked towards her fixing her in a cold and serene gaze.

"What did I just tell you Andreu, see? You just asked me another question." She sobbed.

Andreu smiled concernedly "Mary. Why are you crying?"

"I'm crying because nobody ever in my life has been interested in knowing why I hurt myself." She confessed resisting the urge to look directly into Andreu's eyes.

"And I ask you again, Mary, why? What dark enigmas do you hide? How many layers are you hiding beneath the real woman that lies deep inside you? Why do you think you need to hurt yourself? Let me examine your thigh."

Andreu took an extra step forward; he was now close enough to breathe in her musk. He closed his eyes in order to savor her perfume and then he gently took her right hand. Mary Smith looked at him in surprise. Slowly he then placed his left hand on her neck and pulled her gently towards him. Now Mary could not resist closing her eyes and inhaling his scent of fresh grass and the sea. Andreu smelled of nature. She knew he was about to kiss her and she could have stopped everything, but Mary Smith decided to bring her lips closer to his. He desired her juicy and dangerous mouth. Without hesitation she accepted his lips, then they enjoyed deliciously receiving the flesh of each other's tongues.

Three minutes later there was a knock on the door. Both of them separated immediately. Andreu attempted to tidy Mary's hair while she tried to remove the smears of her pink lipstick from his face with her fingers. They exchanged mischievous smiles, checking that they were both presentable. Andreu lifted her by her waist and sat her on the couch, then quickly tore the plastic wrapping off a dressing and began to bandage her right wrist.

"Come in." Andreu said as he flashed Mary a private grin.

Margaret entered.

"Good afternoon." Margaret greeted them both politely. "Oh What has happened to your arm?" She asked in a worried tone.
'Oh it's nothing serious." Andreu explained despite trying hard to sound serious. "Miss. Smith has a sprained wrist."

26
What is your price?

Out in the corridors of the sixth floor.

"What is the matter Margaret?" Mary asked, trying to conceal her excitement.

"It's very urgent. We have a problem with Carmen Spain." Margaret explained as she followed Mary's steps.

"How come? Her latest novel is selling like hotcakes." Mary replied, while enjoying the secret pleasure of her underwear damp with desire. "Both Carmen Spain and Orlando The Great are nothing but profit for our company."

"Yes but I just talked to Carmen Spain on the phone. Do you remember back in September we commissioned her to write a new book?" Margaret added nervously.

"Of course I remember. I asked her myself because of the record sales of her last novel, *Aliens Love on Earth*. With a second novel we could only increase our dividends." Mary said as she stepped into the elevator.

"Carmen Spain is no longer in New York. She has escaped. She has emptied her bank account; sold all her properties and has gone off to Spain. She literally says she does not want to keep on writing and wants to devote herself to dancing flamenco, gorging on tapas and red wine, and lying down with hot blooded Latins.

133

Basically she has refused to write any more novels because she only wants to live." Margaret concluded with a sigh.

The elevator reached the first floor and Margaret dutifully followed Mary into her office.

"All Right." Mary uttered. "I think I understand her now."
"How do you mean? Margaret asked in disbelief.
"I can certainly understand that one would want to leave and enjoy life." Mary replied with a shrug.
"I don't understand you, Ma'am."
"It's okay, Margaret. You go and enjoy the rest of the day and have a good weekend. You do not need to worry about anything. I will take care of this matter. I'll try to talk to her and convince her, but I can understand her well. Life is just and four miserable letters and fear too short to waste it pointlessly. And now please leave the office and get the hell out of here. You spend too many hours working here in this company."

Mary Smith followed Margaret to the door, ushered her out, shut the door and turned the key in the lock. Margaret stood outside the door as stiff as a statue in the hallway. In all the twenty years she had worked for her boss, this was the first time she had ever ordered her to go home before half past six and advised her to live life without wasting time. She was flabbergasted.

****

Once alone in her office, Mary Smith sat back in her chair and put her feet up on her desk. A quick glance at her bandaged wrist left her roaring with laughter.

"Damned Cuban." She said aloud. "Never in my life have I felt so wet."

It was at this very moment that Andreu knocked at her door. She got up and let him in.

"I have returned." He said as he closed the door behind him.
"How come? She replied staring straight into his blazing naughty eyes.
"I have not finished with your medical examination." He explained with false seriousness.
"Wait a moment." She stopped him coldly. "Before we go any further I need to ask you one question and make a proposal."

Andreu shrugged his shoulders. For him Mary Smith had two modes just like a computer - the "on" mode and the "off" mode. She could go from absolute seriousness or "on" to total loosening up or "off". Definitely at that precise moment Mary Smith was in the "off" mode.

"Tell me how I can help you and what is your proposal."
"I must tell you Andreu that I do not believe in love. Love is a vague concept and too abstract." Mary Smith paused for a moment before continuing. "We call love every feeling that in reality, we do not know how to define precisely. It is simply very difficult to conceptualize it."
"Go on Miss. Smith." Answered Andreu as he crossed his arms.
"Okay. I will start with my proposal. I wanted to propose to you that if you want to be my lover." Andreu was astonished at Mary's bold assertion. "My private elevator has a secret code that you have to enter to get up to my penthouse. The code is "3214smith". If you really want to be my lover, come here on Saturday evening at eight o'clock. Use the code that I have just given you and you will be able to get into my home. If you don't want to be my lover, just don't come. Here is a special electronic pass that will allow you to access the building at any time of day or night and at weekends too."

"I still don't understand whether that's a proposition or a question, but the whole idea is whether I should want to become your lover." He said taking the electronic card and stuffing it into one of his trouser pockets.

"That's correct." Confirmed Mary who had resumed her position with her red soled Louboutin shod feet up on her desk.

"And for how long do you propose I should be your lover?" Andreu stuttered.

"I would only assume tomorrow, that is Saturday for now." She replied in absolute seriousness.

"Only for Saturday?" Andreu was dumbfounded by her candor.

"That's correct." She confirmed.

"Is that not just a little bit mathematical?" He stated still in a state of shock.

"I do not know any other way." She replied.

"Okay. And are there any rules in this kind of contract or proposition?" Andreu asked.

"Of course. You must not hurt me." She explained at which point he started to laugh out loud.

"I can't believe the conversation we are having." He exclaimed.

"Why not?" She said rising from her seat.

"Things shouldn't be done this way, Mary." He rejoined almost with a whimper.

"'I have only made you a proposal which you have yet to accept or reject. I still haven't asked you the question though." She added forcefully.

"Oh, so there is still the question." Andreu replied irritably.

"How much do you want for tomorrow? I assure you that it will only be for a couple of hours. I will not bother you any more than necessary." Mary explained gravely.

"What?" Andreu shouted stretching his neck until he felt a sharp crunch.

"I am only asking you how much I should pay you for your services." Mary explained with such dignity and restraint that Andreu could hardly believe his ears.

Mary looked, eyed him up seriously like a proper businesswoman - as if she was haggling for a product - he stood still so stunned, that he appeared rooted in the virtual soil of the office.

"We must understand each other clearly. What I am asking you for is a categorical answer to my proposal and my question." Mary Smith cocked her head to one side like a curious robot.

Andreu took just one step closer towards her, lent across the desk and with his stringy right hand he slapped her hard on her soft left cheek. The slap was like a crack; she felt a sharp pain and violent burning. Andreu blinded with rage turned around, strode out of the office and slammed the door.

The secret code to enter Mary's penthouse was "3214smith" and that was only the second time in her entire life that she, Mary Smith, had a door slammed on her.

27
Power Game

It was Saturday evening. As the clock struck seven thirty Andreu mopped up the last drops of water that lazily dribbled down his naked torso; the young Cuban was getting ready to visit Mary Smith's Penthouse.

As he got dressed he was unable to control the whirlwind of his emotions. He hadn't slept a wink the night before.

Arriving at the front door of the building, he flashed his electronic pass card to the guard on duty; that same very special card awarded by the queen bee, Mary Smith.

Andreu hesitated for a moment. He didn't know whether he should enter that secret code which had been imprinted into his mind as if his very life depended on it. She had told him: "3214smith " and mind made up, he tapped the code into the keypad. With an almost silent hiss the elevator doors that opened capriciously for her twice daily when she ascended to and descended from the heart of her empire, glided open now before him without hesitation.

Each floor illuminated the display above the door as the elevator climbed to the top of the building and at each stage; Andreu became more and more melancholic, as if the poor boy had had his innocent soul ripped from his body.

"How much was the great lady ready to pay for his services? How much?" he thought to himself

Again and again Mary Smith's words swirled through his head like an angry snake anxious to spit out its poison.

The elevator jerked to a stop, he had arrived at his destination and there was no turning back.

Steeling himself, the Cuban left the elevator car and crossed the deeply carpeted lobby to the single door and knocked. After a disconcerting pause it was opened by a professional woman with a mischievous smile. That smile proved once again that she could get everything that she wanted, provided she paid for the services she demanded. And on that Saturday night the lady wanted nothing more than the burning body of Andreu.

It was Mary who opened the conversation.

"Come in please Andreu. I have been waiting for you. I see you have accepted my proposal and that pleases me very much. I appreciate it greatly."

For a few seconds she let Andreu admire her voluptuous body, wrapped in a very revealing black negligee, but he didn't look for long and instead he returned a pitiful smile.

"But, please, take a seat. Would you like a drink? I have a predisposition for fine Scotch whisky or Bourbon." Mary Smith said as Andreu silently settled into the plush sofa.

Mary carried on with her monologue without noticing Andreu's indifference.

'But, wouldn't you like a drink? I understand that this situation can be tense and perhaps a little embarrassing."

Then the Cuban broke his silence.

"May I ask you a question Mary?"
"Of course."
"What am I to you Mary? What do you think of me having agreed to come here?"

"I understand you now, Andreu, and the reason for your present attitude. I want you to know that I fully understand how you are feeling right now, but if it makes you feel any better, all the men who meet me end up feeling the same way. I think that you need to understand and respect women like me who hold the reins of their own lives." Mary Smith replied savoring the rich scent of her Islay malt whisky.

Mary Smith paused to discover that the words she had just spoken were having no effect upon Andreu, he was looking just as morose as before.

"You still haven't answered my question Mary. What am I to you? Would I be just a sex toy for you if I accept the offer to become your lover?"

"I can assure you that you shall not be my sex toy. It's too cliché these days anyway, don't you think? This is just a simple contract between you and me and no more. You do your job and I will reward you for your services. That's all."

"I got it." Said the Cuban.

Andreu slowly stood up and walked towards Mary Smith who was still sipping her Scotch. Andreu's powerful hand swept through the air to impact on Mary's face and send the crystal glass flying to shatter against the panoramic windows. The slap opened a small wound on her lower lip causing blood to trickle down her chin.

"Who do you think you are that you dare to slap me again? This is the SECOND TIME. You're a fool who has no idea what he has just done."

But then Andreu sealed her mouth with his lips in a passionate kiss. Overcome with his passion Mary let him fill her mouth with the warmth of his saliva.

Softly and slowly, Andreu peeled the delicate transparent negligee from her shoulders as Mary's hands grasped Andreu's back, exploring each and every one of his finely chiseled muscles. A raging passion had been ignited in this lady, who felt that with each of his kisses, she was recovering the spark of her lost youth.

Quickly Andreu's lips moved down to kiss her elegant musk scented neck, as the heat of their bodies seemed to spread all around the room.

Playful and eager to recapture the forgotten thrill of a good orgasm, Mary responded to kisses and the power of his caress. In return she kissed his steely pectorals before dropping to her knees. With a sudden movement, she pulled the belt from his trousers and opened his fly.

With her knees resting on the marble floor Mary smith was ready to draw Andreu's already engrossed member deep into her mouth. But Andreu didn't want that. Grabbing her under the arms he gently lifted her off the ground and held her right in front of him. This time he decided he would be dictating the rules.

Mary was fascinated and ready to let Andreu use her body at his will, which suited the young Cuban.

Andreu's tongue explored the whole expanse of her breasts, finally rotating the tip of his tongue around the areola that surrounded Mary Smith's proud and by now achingly erect nipples. Andreu drew each of them into his mouth and bit them softly, again and again. Enfolded deep within Andreu's arms Mary felt as if she was within a chrysalis, from which she never wanted to emerge.

Mary Smith's nails dug into Andrue's back, as if to confirm that her Adonis was real. Andrue grabbed he buttocks and pulled her towards him, as her legs encircled his waist he thrust her up against the armor-plated glass of the Penthouse's panoramic window. For Mary, it was if his organic weight threatened to crush not just her body, but also each and every one of her absurd concepts about love. He threatened to bring her to an explosive orgasm.

Andreu slipped down her body and now she imagined that she was the one who was about to feel the exquisite pleasure of oral sex. The Cuban had dropped to his knees and with his thumbs he tugged down the final barrier of lingerie that obstructed her sex from his tongue.

On the verge of complete sexual collapse, she threw her right leg over his shoulder and abandoned herself to the raw pleasure of the experience. But despite his passion Andreu was not that experienced and didn't know how to maximize her pleasure, so he just kissed the inside of her thighs and licked those legendary wounds she had inflicted with her nails.

At that distance the perfume of Mary's sex inebriated Andreu's senses, he wanted to devour them like candy. However, with superb self-control, he stopped himself to stand and face Mary Smith. Grabbing both of her wrists in one hand he pinned her arms to the window above her head, and with his free hand, Andreu swept her tawny mane to one side giving him a clear path to her neck and ears which he devoured with his lips and tongue.

Andreu dropped back to his knees to kiss and lick those succulent thighs whose firmness testified the many hours of gym workout invested in them. Mary Smith found herself aroused by these games, unable to control what her body was doing. Her breathing came in almost uncontrollable gasps when his tongue finally probed deep within her lower lips.

The lady had become a mere puppet in the hands of her puppeteer.

Getting up from his knees, Andreu took one of her delicate hands firmly in his and drew it into his shorts so that she could take his manhood between her fingers.

"I want you inside me." Mary whispered plaintively as she stroked his penis with one hand and drew down his trousers and shorts with the other.
"How much?" Andreu demanded.
"I beg your pardon." Replied Mary, as she fought with the buttons of his shirt.
"How much are you willing to pay me to fuck you?"
"Right now however much you ask for." She was mad with desire. "Just tell me how much and it will be yours." Mary Smith gasped.

Andreu pulled away from her, picked up his clothes and turned towards the door dressing as he walked.

"I thought we had a deal." She mumbled.
"That's your problem, Mary, thinking we had a contract." He said as pulled up his trousers. "One more thing Miss. Smith" He said as he pulled on a shoe. "You don't buy caresses." He buttoned his shirt, stuffed the

tails into his trousers and opened the door. "Caresses should be free" He strode across the elevator lobby and pressed the call button. "I am captivated by you. I dream of you every night, but I don't want it this way. I do not want it this way Miss. Smith." The elevator doors hissed opened.

"Please wait a moment." Mary said with her unmistakable earnestness. "We must deal with this like civilized adults. Please come back and sit down, so we can talk this over."

Andreu stood still examining Mary's eyes, they seemed to be now a shade between dark blue and black. Her thick blond hair was disheveled and her expression was as sulky as a cat's. Her nakedness was now covered with her negligee, but she had forgotten to retrieve her panties from the floor. Beckoning him back inside with her hand she invited him to sit down upon the living room couch. He agreed to sit at the place she had indicated and Mary stood in front of him, resting her bottom on an oak table. She crossed her arms as the elevator doors hissed shut.

"Now please tell me what your problem is and we will solve it in a civilized manner." Mary returned to her "off" mode to deliver her sentences. Although clad in the lace trimmed negligee, her naked body showed through, glowing and lustrous, through the flimsy transparency of the fabric and Andreu began to feel the vague presentiment that he had made a bad move by reacting the way he did as if a succulent sweet had been stolen from his mouth.

"Mary, you can't buy caresses, you can't buy love." He explained unable to take his eyes off her sweet and virtuous curves.

"Very well Andreu. I apologize because I have certainly made a mistake." Mary replied rendering him temporarily speechless. "But I need you to explain your problem to me." The forever Mary Smith stated maintaining her characteristic professionalism even with this most delicate of matters.

"I have already told you, Mary. You can't buy or sell caresses. They should be given freely." He stubbornly reiterated his theory of love or friendship, but she was still nonplussed, since she was quite used to paying for such services.

"Let me explain something to you, Andreu." She started to say. "My second ex-husband, Mr. Tomas Davis, was impotent." Andreu couldn't believe his ears and a swirl of hot and cold sweat began to slide down his back as Mary continued her confession. "Tomas made love to me more or less as you have commenced to make love to me." Andreu's eyes widened at Mary's unexpected candor. "He was a man who wanted me to feel that he was fairly attentive with that sweet old tenacity to persuade my body with kisses and caresses." Mary explained as a sweet lascivious expression lit up her face. "But then, Andreu, when the moment arrived, Tomas despaired because despite being so loving and attentive, he was also impotent and in the end, the situation only made both of us extremely frustrated." Andreu was flabbergasted. "So I am asking you now, Andreu, are you impotent or do you go off premature?" Mary Smith expressed her words with absolute seriousness and without any conception that she could cause offense.

"What did you just say?" Andreu shouted as he got up from his seat.

"Please don't slap me again. Mary replied with a cold gaze. "You have already messed up my face enough."

"I will not slap you again Miss. Smith, but can you please repeat to me that little question? I don't think I have understood you." He said trying to work out what Mary was thinking, with her shining damp blue eyes. Her bleeding lips opened once more to repeat the same question for him.

"Are you a powerless man in bed matters?" Reiterated Mary Smith while she tried to withstand withering under Andreu's glare.

Andreu said nothing. He just grabbed her by her hips and slid her bottom back onto the table so that her legs were left hanging off the edge. Andreu didn't want to kiss her; he just looked into her eyes; wanting to study the reaction of this impertinent woman whose opened lips – bloody, pink and wet – displayed her sparkling white teeth. He dropped his trousers and thrusted his swollen member into her - without any preamble. She looked up with lustrous eyes, feeling Andrue's powerful member reaching the deepest part of her being in that one stroke. He lashed into her warm humidity until she could bear it no longer and gave in to her first orgasm. Andreu's face dimpled as he grinned. A deep pleasurable groan emerged from deep within her throat, which further excited Andreu.

She begged him to stop, but he lunged deep into her again; somehow analyzing her emotions at the same time; he wanted to observe how this great lady felt when his powerful member riveted her, right there, until the lady writhed in painful ecstasies. His rock solid member invaded her warm wet sex and she moaned as she gave in to the second wave of orgasms. She begged him to stop again, but he renewed his action, her soft moans betraying that she had succumbed to the overwhelming abyss of pleasure. Her emblematic musky odor pervaded the air in the room and Andreu could not hold himself back any longer. He squeezed his green eyes shut tight as he felt the contractions of her vagina, telling him of the third wave of orgasms hitting the great lady. He grabbed her face and drew her succulent pink lips to his and kissed them roughly, opening up the bleeding wound further as he lunged into her hot dripping cavity and flooded her with his fierce heavy sperm.

28
The memory of Fernanda

With her wet vagina dripping and her shivering body charged with the residue of pleasure, Mary Smith uncoupled herself from Andreu's embrace and leapt from the table. Taking a moment to stretch out back, she turned on her heel and without saying a word, headed towards the bathroom, trying to conceal the fact that her sex was stinging. Their carnal storm had left her sore: her lip was bleeding and itching impertinently, she needed a hot shower.

Left alone in the living room Andreu curled up on the leather upholstery of the couch. Despite the generous proportions of his frame, he still looked like a child on its massive width. He felt the need to detach himself from that recent experience, trying not to perceive the aggressive musky perfume that was still lingering in the air. Fernanda hadn't smelt like Mary. Fernanda had a fresh scent of wet grass and sea. That frenzied clash of these two very different feminine scents stuck in Andreu's mind like printed memory ... together with the last words of Fernanda's love: "I'll always be yours forever."

Those tender words had been etched into his memory and yet, now here he was huddled in the cold white leather of the couch with the boss taking a shower after he had given her three explosive orgasms. The lady was colder than ice and this really irritated Andreu. Not even a kiss as they parted, or any gesture of tenderness or gratitude. The lady had gone - without saying a word, to irrigate her burning private parts with hot water.

Andréu liked to think that Mary wasn't the ice woman she appeared to be. He wanted to believe that she was a tough woman because of her professional life circumstances. He didn't want to just provide her with sessions of lovemaking, but to also offer his love and friendship to her. Andreu wished that what had just happened hadn't been so sordid or sexually explicit. At least they should become friends first. The feeling that Mary would soon come out of the bathroom and say to him, "Thank you very much. You can leave now, I no longer require your services" made him curl up even tighter within the entrails of that cold white leather sofa.

And indeed, Mary emerged from the bathroom wearing a white toweling robe, and was just about to open her mouth when Andreu, taking a single bound from the sofa, was on her. He placed his index finger on her lips as if to beg her not to speak, scared of the heartbreaking phrases she would most likely utter.

"Don't say anything." Andreu said sweetly as Mary's eyes widened. "You don't need to say a word, because if you open your mouth, you will surely say something stupid."

Andreu grabbed the back of her neck with one hand and pulled her towards him. They kissed each other deeply while with his other hand he lifted her robe to caress her smooth rounded bottom.

"And now, is there something you have to say?" He asked her as both hands cupped her curvaceous buttocks. "Would you like to come here again tomorrow, Sunday at four o'clock in the afternoon, I will be in my office on the first floor?"
'That was the right question Mary." He replied. "Don't you want me to stay and sleep with you tonight?" Andreu added with a grin.
"It's many years now since I last slept with anyone." She reddened. "I'm not used to sleeping with people." She recalled the loneliness of her nights with only the cold touch of her sheets.

Andreu's eyes lit up with joy. It seemed to him that the boss was beginning to melt.

"I can't do it." She continued. "You must give me a little time."
"OK." He nodded. "I'll give you some time and I will come back tomorrow at four, but you must get used to the idea that one day we will spend the whole night together and that I will never tire of holding you."

Mary Smith felt a crack appear in the iciness of her frozen heart, and then a drop of gall seemed to emerge from the throbbing organ to slide into her weakened body. Now not only her sex was stinging but also her mutilated soul.

29

In The Office Of Lust

Sunday, February 9, 2014, 4:00 PM

Andreu entered Mary Smith's office without knocking. She was waiting for him, sitting on her desk, in her impeccably ironed white blouse, black knee-length skirt and black Louboutin high heels. There were no words. There were no greetings; Andreu knew that she only wanted sex. Mary Smith was able to offer him her whole body, every fold and crevice, but unable to give him or anyone else for that matter, not even a tiny atom of her heart.

So Andreu lifted her bottom off the desk as he pulled up her skirt to her waist, to expose her beautiful endless legs. With his hard muscular hands he unbuttoned the white blouse, something he had often fantasized about before. Licking his lips, he admired her delicate lacy panties and the white bra, which were all that maintained what little privacy she had left. He gently bit her neck, as he undid that bra, and exposed her breasts their nipples hard and proud due to excitement.

"Yesterday you hurt me." She moaned.
"But you liked it." He said as he looked at her lasciviously.

Then Andreu knelt before his lover, he pulled down her white panties and spread her legs wide so that he could explore the secrets of her sex.

"I've never done this before." He whispered as he slid his tongue into Mary Smith's sex. "I am a novice and you must tell me where you like it most." She moaned as he explored her pink folds with his tongue. "Tell me where you want it the most." Her body began trembling as he licked her central carnal point. "Ah I think this is where you like it the most." He added in between licks.

With absolute devotion Andréu passed his tongue over her labia and parting them concentrated on the tiny peak until she could not stop herself from ejaculating, her vagina throbbed as it contracted and flooded with moisture. Andreu devoured all of that juice as it pored out of her. She writhed on the desktop begging Andreu to split her into two with his hardness.

Andreu stripped off his shirt as he rose from his knees, while his mouth kissed every inch of her skin on the way up, taking a long pause at her breasts and subjecting them to the most exquisite pleasures with his mouth. The ardent and juicy lady before him searched desperately for Andreu's manhood wanting to suck it deep into the glow of her vagina.

Andreu didn't need to be asked twice. He unbuttoned his trousers and rubbed up against Mary Smith's naked body with lust. Such was her heat at that moment that the enraged female daubed her own finger with the nectar of her sex and brought it to her mouth, just to experience that Andreu drank without hesitation and then shared it with her breasts.

Mary twisted out of Andreu's embrace and turned around and scattering papers onto the floor spread her legs wide on the desktop, offering Andreu a view of her beautifully rounded bottom that invited him to penetrate her without any further ado. The sight of her peachy behind with her legs spread wide made Andreu salivate.

Andreu anchored his hands on her waist and kept them there until he flooded her sex with a siesmic torrent of sperm.

Locked together they paused for a few minutes to regain their strength, before the two of them - now accomplices and lovers - concluded their lovemaking with a soft kiss. Mary Smith climbed down from the desk, wobbling slightly as she tried to walk as naturally as her aching body would permit. Discovering that that the desk now looked as if it was the victim of a hurricane, Andreu rubbed his temples and started to tidy up the mess. As Andreu tidied Mary Smith put her clothes back on.

"When will you allow me to sleep with you one night?" He asked tentatively.

"I'm not sure." She replied and she blushed again, as she did not like to show any signs of weakness.

"In this country there are always appointments for everything." He shrugged. "Okay then. Let's make a bloody appointment. Next Saturday February 15 and if you don't grant me that appointment, Miss. Smith, I will not grant you any more of my services for free." He winked at her.

"Bloody Cuban." She said as she laughed.

30
The Check

The second week of February kept Andreu busy with a lot of work. She was on the first floor and he was just along the corridor. Their bodies were missing each other. Both of them had fallen into the same carnal obsession; in that mutual disturbance where there was no apparent love or even friendship, but neither of them seemed to be that worried about it. Tenaciously and persistently they just wanted to be together.

Mary Smith was busy promoting Orlando's The Great second novel: *Mexican Love*. She was also trying repeatedly to convince Carmen Spain to leave Spain and return to USA, and to write another novel, but Carmen's was a rebellious soul. Mary remembered the last time she heard her bawling on the phone...

"Go to hell all of you." Carmen screamed at the top of her lungs. "I want to stay here dancing flamenco and flirting with these Mediterranean men. Go away to fry fritters and leave me alone, super Miss. Mary Smith, and your bloody company."

All these tasks kept Mary Smith busy. However, she felt confined in the solitude of her office and she couldn't help missing Andreu's attentions despite her strict business mind.

She liked to think that she had always been a role model to all of her employees and the audacity, boldness and strength against all adversities in business were infectious. She felt that missing Andreu and fighting against these feelings was a great opportunity to test her own words and policies.

"I want you to go up to the seventh floor, to the accounting department." Mary Smith ordered Margaret who began taking down the instructions in her notebook.

"And I want to you to have a check made payable to Andreu Santa Rosa for $ 400,000 as a form of payment for his services.

"Yes Miss. Smith." Margaret acknowledged without hesitation. "Any thing else?"

"Yes Margaret. From now on I no longer want you to call me Miss. Smith. Just call me Mary." Margaret found her legs began to tremble as Mary explained.

"I'm sorry, what did you say?" Mary's sweet gaze confused the Margaret as she found herself succumbing to such a huge change in Mary's personality.

"Just call me Mary. I think after twenty years of us working together, it is a logical thing to ask." Mary's gaze softened further.

"Yes OK Mary." Margaret smiled back, while a reluctant teardrop rolled down her cheek.

****

On Friday February 14th (Valentine's Day), Andreu received a check for $ 400,000. The sum was more than enough to pay off all his debts in Cuba and maintain the estate of his mother and brothers for over ten years. With the check in his hand he ran to Mary Smith's office and entered without knocking.

"I told you that my caresses couldn't be bought. My caresses are something I want to give to you for free!" He screamed as he slammed the door behind him.
"Use the door latch and sit down please." Not even phased by Andreu's abrupt entry she replied patiently.

Mary flipped a switch on the intercom "Margaret I'm not to be disturbed under any circumstances" she exclaimed.

"Andreu do me the favor of sitting down and listening." She ordered him firmly, but at the same time gently. Mary could not help but notice the pulsating veins in Andreu's swollen neck as he took his seat.
"Bloody hell Mary. I'm about to slap you again." Blew Andreu.
"No please." She said laughing. "My face still hurts from the last time."
"But Mary."
"Andreu." Mary interrupted him dryly. "The check is not a payment for your sexual services, which incidentally, are not as good as you think." She clarified with a grin.
"Really?" Andréu was surprised. "So what is it for?"
"I am aware of your family's problems back in Cuba." Andrue's eyes widened as she confessed with the distinctive professionalism.
"How do you know about that? I have never told you."

"My first ex-husband, Richard Milton, phoned me this week. You remember, the man who asked me to offer you a job." Andreu crossed his arms as Mary began to explain.

"And?"

"During our telephone conversation Richard asked me to help John, who I understand is the father of a friend of yours."

"And?"

"Well Andreu. You told your problem to your friend, your friend told his father, his father told my ex-husband and now my ex husband has just this week told me about it." Mary concluded.

"There you see how news spread." Andreu started to laugh. "Anyway I will not accept your check."

"Andreu, consider it a loan if you prefer and give it back to me whenever you can. This issue is not relevant to me." Mary tilted her head to one side as she spoke.

"Wait a minute." Andreu twisted his head towards her. "Did you just say that you're not satisfied with my sexual services?"

"That's correct. That's what I said." Mary confirmed as Andreu got up and closed the office blinds. "But what are you doing?" Mary asked softly.

"First you call me impotent and now you complain about my sexual services." Andreu whispered excitedly as he dropped his trousers. "Come here to me and I'll show heaven."

They smiled at each other, then they embraced and finally they threw themselves into a serene and elongated kiss. Mary felt another drop of gall expressed from her heart, slide into her and collapse within her body. Aside from the sex the Cuban filled her with supreme joy. Miss. Smith was afraid, very afraid. They were becoming good friends and she never had friends before.

31
Intellect versus heart

Saturday February 15, 2014

At half past eight that evening, in the lift lobby of her private penthouse, Mary Smith could already tell that Andreu was on his way to her. With a low ring the bell of her private elevator announced his arrival.

"Good afternoon Andreu." Mary Smith nodded politely. "You have arrived with admirable punctuality." She looked at him with that cold stare that characterized her -

being always just her. Never allowing her heart to govern her perfect mathematical behavior.

Exasperated Andreu lowered his head and thought sadly about how he was unable to follow her strange world of rigidity and logic. At that precise moment he detested her with all his might, but looking up and gazing into her crystal blue eyes that oozed so much sadness, his hatred evaporated. He felt pity for her and as he inhaled her musky scent he followed her into the living room and sat next to her on the white leather sofa, with the intention of delving into her inner world.

"I think our friendship is progressing slowly." He said as he took her hand. "You seem to have only two fixed ideas in that head of yours." She cocked her head to one side in a robotic gesture as talked. Andreu examined her body, which always enjoyed so much. He knew every inch of the skin that he had kissed, licked or caressed, but not a single inch of her feelings. He had penetrated every physical cavity of the Ice Queen's body, he had possessed her in hundreds of ways, but still Andreu felt that heavy mist clouding his mind.
"What are these two things Andreu? I suppose you've made a proper diagnosis of me before venturing to open your mouth." Mary Smith pronounced in her most

professional tone. The one that she thought was so appropriate in the circumstances.

"Work and sex, work and sex and in that precise order, Mary." Andreu quickly replied.

"You are not wrong." She answered politely. "That is the correct order and as for you, I like to feel you and have you."

"But let me know you, Mary." He implored with sudden passion as his passion rose. This impersonal sexual relationship where friendship was so tenuous or even nonexistent irritated him.

"What for Andreu?" She indifferently asked.

"Let me show you that I can also be your friend." He replied with desperation clear in his voice. "Look Mary, I have the fortune to possess you and be there for you at present, but I also want to show you that friendship is possible between us."

"I also like to kiss you, touch you and abandon myself to passion." She confusedly responded.

"Sex Mary, only sex." He said as he lowered his eyes to stare at the pattern on the carpet again.

"So what?" She sighed pretending not to understand.

Andreu felt as if within his mind, one of his neural pieces had erupted and burst into flames. Two furtive tears escaped from his eyes and fell gracefully down onto the curve of his cheekbones. Mary noticed those teardrops, as they remained motionless, without any intention to move. Andreu dropped his pants as those tears began descending and Mary watched how he stuck out his tongue to drink them. Then he placed his erect member between her lips and she closed them around him. Still angry, he felt his manhood swelling in the warmth of her mouth. Once his member had lengthened and broadened to its fullest extent, he unceremoniously grabbed her and flipped her around into the position of a bitch as he pulled up her skirt and moved her panties aside so he could penetrate her anus, without any preambles or warning.

Mary's cries of pain echoed dryly around the room as he was lunging into her, until one of his hard hands stopped her mouth. The wet touch of the tears that cascaded from the terrified eyes of Mary Smith on that hand drove him back and as he looked down that hand wetted with her tears, Andreu wept too. The two separated from their carnal connection and sobbed quietly until he embraced her body with all his might and she allowed the embrace as she quietly wept into his chest.

'Mary I'm sorry. I'm so sorry. Have I hurt you?" Andreu felt remorseful and guilty.

"Don't worry." The teardrops had dampened her face, like a white handkerchief, wet and torn. "I'm used to pain. In fact, I need the pain. It reminds me that I am worthless and that I must suffer."

"The same way you hurt yourself pinching your thigh." He said and she just nodded. "Why Mary?"

"Because I do not deserve to have anyone love me." She replied wrestling herself away from his embrace. "No one has ever loved me. My parents never did, my lovers and husbands didn't either, but I am human at the end of the day, and if I can't receive love from anyone, at least I need them to give me something. I need to get some feelings from others, even if it is only sex or pain. I want you to penetrate me again. I want you to hurt me until I bleed because then at least I will have received something from you."

Andreu lifted her in his arms and carried her gently to the bedroom. He placed her with infinite softness in her bed.

"I will never harm you again, my friend. I never will. I'm sorry about what I have done to you and believe me the memory of this experience will haunt me like a ghost for the rest of my life." Andreu realized that his hand was wet and sticky. Raising his hand to look at it he blanched in terror, the hand was covered in blood. Terrified he discovered a trickle of blood steadily flowing out of her impregnating the white sheets with its red stain.

"I do not care." She said and laughed as if it were a joke. "I do not care if I die bleeding. At least I have received something from you. At least you gave me something. And now let me go. I need to go to the bathroom to wash up and then change the sheets for clean ones."
"No. I am not going to let you leave." He moaned sadly. "Forget about the bloody sheets." He said compressing the wound to her anus with the palm of his hand. "You are not going to waste your time any more without knowing what it is to love or be loved; without knowing what friendship is. You must let yourself go by your heart. Let me be your friend."

Chapter Zero
The Obsessive Regression

But what can you do when eroticism becomes an obsession? What happens when two people without even knowing why or how – meet and between them an obsessive and uncontrollable sexual neurosis develops? How can we judge these two beings that are no longer in control of their actions, since between them a mental representation has become fixed? And after their lewd and disturbing encounters, the pair of them irremediably fall into a world of anguish and anger; doubt, remorse and guilt. Is any form of friendship in the strict sense of the word possible between them? A kind of link had joined them but it was not that of friendship, but rather shared pain instead.

She begged him not to judge her because she couldn't even understand herself. She implored him daily to penetrate her, to open her into two halves, to martyr her flesh; she stubbornly wanted to be, for the rest of her life, chained to that bed, so that Andreu could complete her.

He, meanwhile, participated in that obsession, always mutual and consensual, without understanding the reason for the continuous search for long and embittered orgasms. With the uncertain light of the New York dawn they opened their eyes discovering that their escalation of "gasps" and "groans" would end in a single climax for him, but many more for his lady who belonged to the privileged sector of the female gender: the two percent (according the statistics) who are the multi orgasmic female. She was obsessed with reaching the ascending number of climaxes and he just wanted to see her enjoy her reaching them. She was obsessed with the feeling and he was obsessed with seeing her feel that way. It made him feel like the big and powerful God of the flesh.

****

However, sex is just one miserable personal objective and it varies depending on the individual. After all, everyone manages to join all those pieces of his sexual puzzle together to get that last physical point. We can therefore conclude that the sketches of each person or his different techniques to reach the "deep end" to which we all surrender without resistance - are always the same.

****

Up to now we may all agree, but then what can a female do (as in the case of Mary Smith) who for her weakness (or even disease) is deprived of all her might, with that situation she finds herself, almost handcuffed to her sexual obsession, unable to face his torment and stop the continuous degeneration of her every mental and physical orgasm?

Mary Smith and Andreu were suffering from the world of darkness fuelled by sexual obsession where orgasms daily contracted and expanded to the sound of their bodies, like the indestructible power of a storm of irresistible force.

It is difficult to understand them. Of course they both felt the physical orgasms like any other being, but unlike other mortals, they both also suffered from the obsession to reach them.

Their orgasms began to happen in their own minds. For her it was like a cyclopean phallus, which penetrated even her brain, and after the deep mental indentation, she finished with an explosive outburst of mental fluids. To Andreu all those experiences - sometimes torturous - began to make a dent in his soul and he silently wondered to himself when would he descend into that sexual trap where he would see himself consumed forever.

The problem arose when that overpowering need for each other became the sole purpose of their lives. Every day without resistance, new experiments were carried out.

Andreu tried to rebel against the eternal damnation of his obsession, and from the depths of his inner world he struggled to free himself, but every attempt was in vain because Mary was encrypted into his mind and body. Reaching the heights of those endless orgasms, the obsession threatened his very existence. He realized his terrible sickness was to continue drilling the body and soul of Mary Smith for the rest of his life.

She, meanwhile, was handcuffed, with no possible escape, being penetrated again and again - in all forms and in all manners. She was hopelessly trapped in that phenomenon which consumed her daily.

When she opened her eyes and heard his footsteps, she tried to untie herself, but she couldn't. She always begged him not to tie her up, but she couldn't resist, because she was always hungry of him. Her body and soul told her that Andreu would give her all the food she needed.

32

The ancient oak tree struck and splintered into shards

The situation became untenable, though it persisted through an obsessive February and then a pathological March, during which Andreu learned a little more about Mary Smith (but not much more). He discovered that Mary was - like any other human being - just a product of her circumstances. In any case their sexual relationship intensified becoming true physical torture, where nothing mattered any longer; one day it was a knife slitting her buttocks, the next penetration with foreign objects.

The sick April passed by and then the bloody May and Mary Smith was transmuted into another human character forever obsessive and compulsive, which explained her resultant personality perfectly well. Her parents had never shown her any affection. They had only cared to provide her with the most excellent education. She had governesses and attended the best private schools, but she had grown up alone, like a tenacious and rigid ancient oak. From time to time she wished her oak to be struck by lightning and blasted into splinters. She wanted to see her own wounded trunk being hacked though still deeply rooted in the soil, the same as those harsh and rigorous human beings who hide their hearts beneath a layer of cynicism and realism.

And finally the painful June went by, then the chronic July, then the morbid August and finally came September, the most unjust of all months when Andreu could bear the situation no longer.

"I must return to Cuba." Andreu said and Mary felt heartbroken. She wondered at that moment if it had been worthwhile to end up loving Andreu so foolishly. Despite their atrocious sexual life, she, even with her own chaotic psychology- loved him.
Wouldn't it have been better to have kept a uniquely carnal relationship, plain and simple and with payment included throughout all those months rather than allowing herself to fall in love with him? Had she done it that way, she wouldn't now be feeling her heart torn and the torrent of gall that inundated her entire body. She had fallen in love, in its basic and crude form, because having never having received love from anyone in the past, her soul was filled with the pain he inflicted upon her, and for her this was love. For Andreu, however, those experiences tormented him and he couldn't understand why, because on the one hand, he hated himself for being the violator of her body, but on the other hand he also enjoyed it. It was as if he were two people in one body. It was as if one half of Andreu was

the good man, kind and humane, but his other half was dark with its perverse hidden sexuality.

"I have to go." He repeated. "I'll write. I'll call you." He said because he knew he could never get rid of Mary. She was his soul mate in that sexual obsession.

It was as if the two of them had shared the same trip together and now she had to end her journey alone. The separation was approaching - Andréu was leaving - and she was left alone again, waiting at the bus stop.

"If you must leave, just go." She stated without even a tremor in her voice. "If you ever come back, you know where I am."

Andreu analyzed Mary's behavior – the lady was a specialist in personal torture and mutilation – she was returning to her original self, once again the woman of steel.

"Will you not give me a goodbye kiss? Are not you going to wish me good luck?" Whispered Andreu as he stood up in the silence of the room.
"The best of luck, my friend." She shook her head. "And now, please leave." She added firmly.

Andreu turned around, walked out and slammed the office door.

With a clear head and making best use of her intellect, Mary got up from her swivel chair and walked to the window where she beheld an autumnal New York that seemed to be made of plastic. At that moment, her office door was opened once again and the trembling figure of Andreu was outlined in the doorway.

"You will always be my friend Mary and I'll never stop loving you." He knew that his words wouldn't penetrate the hard shell of Mary Smith.
"And I will always keep the same secret code for my elevator in case one day you decide to return." She replied as she turned her back on him. "And now, will you please leave? I have a lot of work to do."

PART THREE: LOVE AND DEATH

My gut-wrenching love, my death-in-life,

In vain I wait for you to write me a letter,

Like a withered flower I think rather than to live

Without being me, to lose you would be better.

The air is everlasting; the lifeless stone

Neither knows the shade nor shuns the gloom.

The innermost heart doesn't need the frozen

Honey that comes pouring from the moon.

But I suffered for you; ripped my veins,

A tiger and dove wrapped your waist

In a tussle of bites and lilies.

So now fill with words my madness
or let me live in the tranquil
night of my soul, forever in darkness.

English translation by Paul Archer of Lorca's El poeta pide a su amor que le escriba.
Sonnets of Dark Love.

33
No Return

For days in advance, Andreu's friends and relatives were eagerly anticipating his arrival and they were all really excited. Ivan and The Never Doer were yearning to take Andreu out for a drive in the old Cadillac, taking a trip through the quiet streets of Havana once more – just like they had done so many times in the past.

The "mater familias" of the Santa Rosa clan felt grief in her heart knowing that her beloved son was returning home. Sarita, his eldest sister, found herself in an emotional dilemma because although Andreu's return filled her with joy, it was a problem for her to tell him that she had a boyfriend; the very thought of doing so made her hands sweat profusely.

For his younger brothers, Jasmine and Justin, the prospect of Andreu's return was like that of a father coming back home.

From the plane Andreu could see how the infinite blue sea capriciously surrounded the majestic island of his birth. On landing even before setting foot on solid ground, some tourists, seduced by Cuba's magic, were already firing the flashes of their cameras.

But no one in Bayamo overflowed with such joy as much as Fernanda did. She anxiously counted the seconds to when she would see that pair of green eyes. Eyes that could look so deeply into her that they could undress her soul. Fernanda had prepared a warm welcome for Andreu after his long year of his absence.

The Santa Rosa's house had been decorated with multicolored paper. The dining room table strained under the weight of the food Fernanda had prepared: there were several different rice dishes and Andreu's favorite dish of roast suckling pig. All this was accompanied by pitchers of 'mojitos', without which no Cuban meal was complete.

Ivan and Sarita had volunteered to meet Andreu at the airport in Havana, while Socorro completed the preparations for the party and got ready to receive the guests.

One by one the whole of the neighborhood managed to cram into the residence of the Santa Rosa, which had it not been for the generosity of the cold Mary Smith, would never have been in a fit state to hold such a celebration.

Andreu felt a tinge of guilt about having abandoned Mary Smith, leaving her vulnerable to whatever fate befell her in the unfriendly and impersonal city of New York. Her parting words still echoed in Andreu's memory. After trying his best over the past seven months to melt her icy heart, he had truthfully achieved very little of that objective, The experience though had changed him for the rest of his life, he would never again be the same Andreu that he had once been.

After all the painful episodes they had gone through, she was still hurting from the invisible wounds he had inflicted upon her. And she had decided, after Andreu's departure, to keep opening them up as indelible reminders of all the attention that the young man had lavished upon her, making her feel a little bit loved. And thanks to the darkness of their experiments, the two of them would always retain those wounds and mutilations.

When she had learned of his departure, the many years of corporate meetings and media interviews had granted her the necessary experience of how to preserve the perfect unemotional mask of the great businesswoman.

She showed the world that nothing mattered to her and that in fact, it was all part of her original plan; she had always known that her affair with Andreu would come to an end.

She had just wished him the best of luck and reminded him of the code for her private elevator. That was what she told him, but inside she wanted to call him back and shout desperately that she would to do anything to keep him with her. It was he and only he who in the entire world that had been able – like a tiny raindrop - to find the chink in her hardened heart. Between experiment and experiment in their lovemaking she had fallen in love with him, but in the process he ended up hating himself, for not controlling the situation and letting himself go.

With his urgent desire to avoid hurting her, Andreu had never been aware of Mary Smith's love for him, as he left, crestfallen, for his beloved Cuba, still believing that he had never been able to penetrate the icy fortress named Mary Smith.

34
Back home

At 2:45pm the flying colossus descended onto the socialist soil, promising a pleasant stay to all of its tourist passengers, but for Andreu coming home was a balm of peace, necessary for him to regain the sanity he had lost while abroad.

Sarita was anxiously waving her hand to her clueless brother at the arrivals, but it was only when his friend and neighbor Ivan stepped up and raised his long arm over the heads of the crowd milling about the arrivals hall, that Andreu became aware of their presence. A warm embrace between the three of them allowed Andreu to taste the love and friendship of the past without any obsessions or delusions once more.

"You don't know how much we have missed you." Slender Sarita said in between plastering her dear brother with kisses.

More laughter, hugs and kisses loaded with euphoria came as Ivan welcomed Andreu; he even offered to carry his friend's luggage.

"Since when have you've been so helpful? You have never carried anything for me in the past." Andreu laughed.

"But tell me, how was it in the United States?" Ivan asked. "Sure you met many pretty girls, of all flavors and colors, right?"

But Ivan's bold comment earned him a sharp elbow in the ribs, courtesy of Sarita. Both of them realized that Ivan's joke far from making Andreu laugh had made him sad.

"Andreu, are you okay?" Sarita asked with concern showing on her face.
"Yes darling. Why shouldn't I be?" Andreu responded, but he couldn't stop thinking that he had left some unfinished business in Mary Smith's empire of romance. The pages of Mary Smith's books sold the most beautiful of loves and yet in his opinion they had never instilled any concept of love in their Ice Queen. Andreu was not aware that his Ice Queen already knew what love was because she was in love with him.

Andreu changed the subject.

"And where is Mama Socorro? Why hasn't she come to the airport?"
"She is at home preparing a meal to celebrate your return. You know how she is. She wants everything to be

perfect before the arrival of her prodigal son." A chuckle escaped from Sarita's lips and Andreu could not resist grabbing her by the neck and kissing his sister on both of her cheeks.

It was a delight for Andreu to start the engine of the old Cadillac, but it was Ivan who sat in the driving seat. With his chin resting on his hand, Andreu admired the beauty of his island, but his moment of reflection was not deep enough for him not to perceive the nervous glances that his sister and Ivan exchanged.

"Let's see. Can you please tell me what's going on between the pair of you? What game are you playing? Even though I've been absent for a year, I haven't forgotten how to tell when something is fishy."

The comment made Andreu's sister nervous. Andreu kept his eyes fixed on Sarita; he was worried that both his friend and his sister were hiding some serious matter.

"Come on spit it out, damn. What is it?" Andreu asked impatiently.

Ivan braked suddenly and pulled the old vehicle to the side of the road, only then was he prepared to release his tongue.

"Look Andreu. You and I have always been very good friends and we have always been honest with each other, right? Well, sincerely I must tell you that Sarita and I love each other and that we have been engaged since March and I love her ... and well ... that if you let me I'll take care of her and respect her. You know I am a man of my word and the truth of the matter is that Sarita will only consent to marry me if you give us your permission."

A silent and awkward moment descended upon the old Cadillac, only to be cut by Andreu's loud laughter.

35
Orlando The Great

Late September 2014

Mary Smith had read and reread Orlando The Great's second novel and after going through editors, translators and more editors, Mexican Love had finally been launched and achieved the massive sales Mary Smith had predicted. She knew it would do well from the moment that the manuscript had landed in her hands. His story line had bewitched her mutilated brain; it was a runaway Bestseller. 'Latinos knew better than anybody else how to make the readers fall in love with their hot stories' she thought.

When Orlando The Great arrived at Mary Smith's offices and met the boss for the first time, his legs were trembling with nerves and his eyes were as wide as saucers.

"I do not believe you are Mary Smith." He gasped. "I thought you would be much older and uglier."

Mary Smith burst out laughing. After getting to know Andreu intimately she was already familiar with the Latin temperament and the reaction of the Mexican writer had not caught her by surprise.

"Sit down please and let me congratulate you." She said smiling sincerely "Ma'am." Exclaimed Orlando The Great. "You can give me whatever pleases you. Believe me, anything you give me, I receive it gladly."

The playful phrases of Orlando made Mary Smith sad because they reminded her of the Cuban.

"Well. Let's focus." She said as she cleared her throat.

"Madam, believe me I'm already very focused." The Mexican replied.

"Shut up for once, please." Mary burst into peals of laughter. "You are not letting me concentrate."

"I have the same problem. " interrupted the Mexican. "I've been puzzled since I've seen you."

"Can we talk seriously, please?" Mary said as she tucked an errant lock of hair behind her ear.

"Tell me." Orlando whispered resting his elbows on Mary's desk as he leaned forward and fixed his gaze on Mary's eyes. "I'm all ears."

"You remind me very much of a Cuban I once met." She shook her head slowly from side to side as she offered up this confession.

"Cuban, Mexican, we are all the same. I hope he was as handsome as me." Orlando guffawed.

"No, believe me." Mary chuckled. "The Cuban was more handsome."

"But surely he was not as funny as I."

"Do shut up Orlando." Mary could not stop herself from roaring with laughter.

"Okay I Shut up."

"Well." Mary took a deep breath. "Your book has become our number one bestseller globally. With "Mexican Love" your sales have overtaken Carmen Spain's."

"Carmen Spain?" Orlando questioned curiously. "What has happened to her? Is she not the lady who wrote that novel about two aliens, who disguised as humans, fornicated in every corner of planet earth?"

"That's correct. It was her who wrote it. Carmen Spain has decided to retire to Spain and will not be writing any more." Mary explained. "Maybe you can help me with that. Now that you're going off to Spain on a promotional tour for your second novel, you could go and see her and try to convince her to continue writing." Mary said as she handed a card to him.

Orlando The Great took a quick glance at the card.

Carmenspain@ntlworld.com

"Very well." The Mexican agreed with a grin. "I'll try to talk to her, I promise, but now let's forget about Carmen, Tell me why don't you and I get together somewhere nice and get to know each other a little bit better?"

Mary Smith put on a grim smile, shook her head and chortled.

"Forget about it, Orlando. I prefer the memory of my Cuban."

36
My shelter

The palpable tension in the Cadillac, between Andreu's oldest friend and his sister over keeping their relationship a secret, had by now vanished, but Andreu felt as if he had been hit on his head. "Who was he to condemn to them?" With a gentle shrug and an inaudible sigh he simply said: "congratulations."

And indeed, who was he to tell them anything? How could he break free from the chain of his own memories? The worst of it was that he didn't believe that his relationship with Mary Smith had been at all wrong. It was true that he had needed to hide it from everyone, (the lady had corrupted his soul for the rest of his life and he would never be the same Andreu again.) And because this was true, he was now forever chained to vice: the vice to seek out the latent greatness of 'the forbidden' for the rest of his life. He tried to throw a hypothesis in his mind to calm himself down, apologizing for his "youthful weakness," but he knew that that idea could only be buried deep in the cemetery of his crazy excuses. The truth and the whole truth was that Mary Smith was like the final cigarette a confirmed smoker intends to smoke for that very last time and therefore it tastes that much more intense because it is the last one.

****

The gathering at the Santa Rosa's home was much more animated than Andreu's sluggish mental state. The place was electric with the positive energy of dancing and laughing friends and relatives. Although Andreu appeared cheerful and amicably conversed with all about his USA adventures, placing special emphasis on his two best American friends, Johan and Patrick, it was Socorro who detected a hint of sadness in her son.

"What's wrong Andreu? What is it that is hurting you so much?" Socorro asked her child as she took hold of his hands. "I love you so much Andreu."
"Everything is good mama Socorro, everything is good. I guess it's the flying that hasn't done me well." Andreu

answered as he tried to conceal the poison that run through his veins.

"But Andreu, do not teach the evil how to do evil things." Socorro replied patiently. "Do you think that the pain of my children can go unnoticed before my very eyes? I'll spare the excuses that are coming out of your mouth. What you have is not physical pain or fear of heights; your pain comes from within. And right now it is better that you don't think about it, but do not forget the advice from your mother. The faster your inner poison disappears, the faster you will cure your soul."

Andreu's sad smile proved to Socorro that her mother's intuition had been right, so with a big hug and a tender kiss he sealed the unwritten commitment that he had made with his mother.

****

As dusk fell the vivid brown colors began to envelope the clear blue Cuban sky. Now dressed in lighter clothes, but with a cold attitude Andreu took off for his refuge. When he arrived the virginal Fernanda was waiting for him. The fabric of her floral print dress was capriciously fluttering against her skin. The sea breeze coming off the heart of the Caribbean had become a satyr to Fernanda's body and threatened to lift her skirt more than necessary.

37
The card

Meanwhile back in New York, a tall emaciated figure that exuded an overwhelmingly strong odor of "hot dogs" stood in Andreu's former apartment with his little eyes wide open, as he projected his flashlight into the darkness seeking out where the light switch could be.

He had been watching Andreu closely, very closely. Almost every day he would have greeted him twice. The first of these greetings always left him with a few extra dollars in his pocket and Andreu with a tasty breakfast of spicy hot dog with lots of onion. Every morning after breakfast Andreu would run the circuit of Central Park, which kept him in great shape. So, little by little, day-by-day, the hot dog man observed the situation carefully, listening to Andreu's stories and methodically filing away the information he gained. He had discovered that Andreu worked in Miss MS Editorial and that he lived in the apartment of a friend who he had met at college. And so in this manner, the long patient Hotdog Man had collected all the information he needed, added all the clues together and deduced the most opportune time to pit his plan into operation. At the end of the day he was just a simple hot dog man and given the paucity of his salary, there were times he had to pursue "other occupations."

And that was the reason he was there searching for the bloody light switch. At the precise moment he found it, he hastened to locate any valuables he could find. He knew the apartment was unoccupied, since Andreu had innocently informed him that he was going away. Andreu was ignorant of the consequences that his innocent words could lead to and the cunning figure knew he had all the time in the world to search, though it wasn't a matter of doing things slowly either.

With absolute coldness, he remembered the sincere laughter of the innocent Cuban, always so cheerful, so ... innocent. Although it was true that over time he saw Andreu change and after a few months in New York, he had became a little more "introverted" or maybe a little more "dark".

Hotdog Man shrugged his shoulders as his eyes scanned every inch of the apartment. The gold jewelry and diamonds inside one of the drawers of the main bedroom were handsome enough and the ridiculous safety box with cash inside was also good. Although he did think that $ 5,000 was not an extravagant sum of money to be kept in such a luxurious Central Park apartment. So the hot dog fragranced figure resumed the arduous task of plundering this easy and safe ground. He searched every nook and cranny of the apartment over two long hours until he reached the guest room, the one which Andreu had been using during his stay at there.

As he entered he cast a swift glance around the room and then took a deep sniff. He laughed when he realized with absolute certainty that it was Andreu's room. Feeling pleased that he had finally found the room that he was hunting for, he didn't think twice before he began opening all the drawers and cupboards.

As he pulled the handle of the top drawer of the bedside table, he did it with such force that the drawer emptied its contents onto the floor, displaying just two objects before his greedy eyes.

The burglar carefully slid the drawer back into the table and examined the two objects with interest: one was an electronic key card for entry into Miss MS' Editorial and the other was a tiny slip of paper with 3214smith written upon it. Hotdog Man's curiosity was fired: "3214smith".

He stuffed both objects into his pockets and grabbed the backpack he had filled with all the other valuables he had taken. Taking time to pull up his gloves and pull down the brim of his black hat, he pocketed his flashlight and turned off the lights. Then he vanished like a rat into the dark.

Outside it was cold and drizzling. Everything was unpleasant and gloomy but the burglar was the happiest man on earth. Deep inside in his mind he was conceiving the most perfect of plans.

38
My Refuge (continuation)

With eager steps, the two lovers returned to the place where they had played Romeo and Juliet so many months before. . Standing opposite one another with their feet firmly positioned on the beautiful soft sand. Fernanda's body was both soft and warm.

There was an extra essence in Fernanda's characteristic fragrance that evening. A perfume that Andreu could not decipher, at least not in the short term. But it was undoubtedly familiar. After all the sublime experiences with Mary Smith, Andreu had learned to smell the flesh and feel with every pore of his skin. The usually prohibited practices between human beings create a kind of wisdom without decorum. And for this reason Andreu had discovered the bewitching scent of Fernanda. She smelled of excitement and Andréu was ashamed because he thought it was obscene that there was no point of return, for he could never be to her what he was once before.

Their seemingly timeless embrace was followed by Fernanda's soft kiss. She had the firm intention of provoking in Andreu the desire to stay longer as he savored her full lips. And without slowing down her well-studied plan, she broke free from him and ran across the border that divided the sea from the sand, forcing Andreu to pursue her in a game that had long been played in the past by these two secret lovers. He couldn't help enjoying the scent of her shameless excitement.

Eventually, he caught up wit her and grabbed her fragile body; Fernanda fell like a prey animal to his impetuosity. He was playing the role of the hunter of that perfume. And this was an ironic thing because there is no woman who can't bring her man to the ground. It is the woman with her sweet smile who injects her warm poison, not through a sharp sting, but softly with her crimson lips.

Fernanda dragged Andreu down into the sparkling clear waters of the Caribbean; Fernanda's firm breasts become immediately visible beneath the now translucent fabric of her wet dress, clearly displaying her beautiful hard nipples. This did not go unnoticed to Andreu's thirsty eyes and it was at this point that that Fernanda was revealed as the wolf disguised as a sheep. Drawing her hair back away from her face, she let him have a full free view, a present only for his eyes.

Beautiful Fernanda was the distillation of erotic excitement and she clinched Andreu close to her, rubbing her wet breasts against Andreu's torso, his muscles perfectly outlined behind the damp cotton shirt. Their mouths closed upon each other's as they met in a long and passionate kiss.

It was she who broke the silence.

"Did you like it Andreu?"
"Very much." He answered inhaling her scent.
"How much?" She asked passionately.
"To the point of wanting to kiss you and hold you every day for the rest of my life."

She was pleased with his answer, and without saying a word, she took his hand to go back to Mamas Socorro's house so that they could continue to enjoy his homecoming party, both thankful to the waters of the sea for concealing their wet excitement - a product of that erotic game.

They were back in that old porch where they had once drunk together for the last time, when she whispered.

'What happened today is nothing compared to what will happen tomorrow at midnight. And please be punctual. I have been waiting for you for a whole year."

Once said, Fernanda went back into the house returning to her innocent personality as if nothing had happened. Andreu stood there motionless as his eyes followed the rhythmic sway of her hips.

****

A night of passion. The following night Fernanda nervously got herself ready for what would be her perfect romantic night by choosing her most seductive underwear. Her shapely toned young body was capable of awakening the most ardent sexual fantasies in any man - although she was only interested in one man and that was Andreu.

With a body pure in every sense of the word, she hid herself under her sheets, impatiently waiting for the arrival of her Romeo, but the caprice of fate had preyed on her once again. She was such a beautiful woman, but no matter how beautiful she was or how great her love was for Andreu, she waited for him in vain all through that long sultry night. As the time drew on she raged with anger in that solitary bed unable to satisfy the overwhelming desire to be fulfilled between her legs.

For his part Andreu didn't sleep either that night or on many other nights. Fernanda couldn't understand why he had rejected her so categorically.

39
The first and last call

Saturday 13th September: "I wanted to call you." Andreu said. "I wanted to hear your voice. I miss you so much, you know? Today is Saturday." He took a deep breath and she held hers. "Every Saturday I would take you in my arms and in that moment you always became another kind of woman, more friendly and loving. How are you Mary?"
"As usual." She replied the tone of her voice low. "Although I do miss you too." Mary added," You have not explained to me yet why you had to return to Cuba so suddenly."
"They needed me here." He answered quickly.
"I see." Mary remained silent for a long time. "Or was it you that needed them?"

"New York was exhausting." He said trying to skirt around the question. "I still have a clouded mind. I am still very confused." He added rapidly without pausing to take breath.

"No Andreu." Mary affirmed with her characteristic authority. "You were always willing to be submissive to me, as I was to you, but you were looking for your opportunity to leave me. You have simply taken advantage of the most favorable time to return to Cuba and be with your people."

"And yet." He whispered as he mopped the sweat from his forehead. "You are stuck in my head and in my skin for the rest of my life. You do not know how many times I have come close to catching the first plane out of here to be with you."

At that precise moment, Mary Smith's living room was dimly lit, but despite the gloom as Mary took a sip of Scotch from her glass with the phone cradled between her ear and her shoulder, she noticed a shadow projected on to the marble floor.

"Tell me that you love me." She coldly commanded.

Andreu really wanted to confess her that at that precise time, he didn't love her and that he never had done. He had always been in love with Fernanda, but he didn't want to hurt Mary any more.

"I love you with all my soul and all my heart. You'll always be my queen." Andreu lied as he hid his face in his hands. "Now you tell me."
"I love you. Of course I love you and I love you more than I've never loved anyone in this world, and you know why, do you know why my dear friend and lover? Because you taught me how to love." Mary's cold voice broke as she concluded.

The only light in the living room gave a reddish hue to the face of the assailant behind her as he struck a blow to Mary's head. As she crumpled to the floor she turned her head to fix her crystal blue eyes onto him, bathed in the reflected scarlet light he seemed to be the devil himself.

A stream of blood gushed from her head and pooled around her. She stared at him as he stood over her, his head cocked to one side as he watched her die, despite the final spasms as death crept up on her Mary noticed that although she did not recognize his face, he stank of hot dogs.

The telephone handset had fallen on the floor beside her.

"Mary ... Mary ..." Andreu lamented on the other side of the line.

With the methodical precision of a cold blooded killer Hotdog Man picked up the handset and returned it to its cradle.

Mary Smith's body convulsed with the final spasms of death. On the other end of the line Andreu heard the screeching whistle that told him the line had been cut off. Hotdog Man took a final look at Mary; her eyes were wide open and her head was surrounded by a halo of blood. She was a beautiful blond woman with a musical smile: the smile of one who has accepted her imminent end.

Those last few seconds had been the longest of her life. She only wished that Andreu could have held her at the end, had caressed her with his tough and tender fingers one last time. She only wished that her lover and friend could have (just for the last time) have shown her the ecstatic sweetness of a love so tender that it could have flooded her tortured heart before the end.

40

The memory of the last cry

Andreu never imagined that Mary Smith had been killed; on the contrary he believed that her last groans were some kind of a tasteless joke. He even reflected that her climatic last cry must have been the product of a new lover, perhaps a Brazilian or maybe an Italian. The truth of the matter for Andreu seemed to be that the lady must have invited another man into her castle to satisfy her burning desires. Andreu was almost certain that this must be the case since every time the lady reached an orgasm, she sobbed as if she was dying.

****

It was the first Thursday of October and Socorro burst into Andreu's room, to finish the conversation that had been pending from the day of his return.

"May I enter?" The opening words of his mother were naturally irrelevant as without waiting for his answer, she closed the door behind her.
"Go ahead." Andreu smiled, since he knew that no matter what he had answered, his mother would have entered anyway.

Socorro stood at the doorway and watched her son as he sat by the window. He looked as if he was spying on people in the neighborhood - just to have something to do to justify his existence.

"What happens Andreu?" Socorro asked.
"Nothing mother, what could possibly happen to me? I'm back home and that's more than I could ask for."
"Really Andreu? Do you really think you can get away again? The Andreu I know would now be very happy enjoying life with his friends, making a campfire or playing the guitar. The Andreu I know would be taking care of his sisters and correcting his younger brother, who regardless of his naughty behavior and pranks, would still love him unconditionally."
"What do you want me to tell you, mother? Perhaps I have changed. Have you thought that maybe I'm not the same Andreu that I was before I left for America?" He rebuked her through all the upset and hurt that the felt.
"Yeah, I guess that all of us change over the years, but the change should be for the best my love, and no change is good when a nice young man like you lets that girl with the long braids with whom you grew up and fell in love with, weep on her own. Have you thought that you might have left her at the mercy of the arms of another man?"

Socorro's comment made Andreu turn his face his mother with an expression that was a picture of doubt.

"What do you know about her? Has she said something to you? Have you seen her? Has she got a new boyfriend?" His barrage of questions made him look desperate, but all Socorro could say to reassure him was "She hasn't told me anything. I haven't seen her, but certainly I know that if you do not fight for Fernanda, you are just throwing her into the arms of another man."
"Perhaps it would be better." Andreu replied. "She deserves to be with someone better."
"Better than whom? Socorro countered.
"Better than me, of course." Andreu answered.
"But love is not a matter of being better than anyone. Love is knowing how to choose who you want to share your life with."

Andreu's gaze returned to the streets of Bayamo, so Socorro opted to leave the room, but as she busied herself with her chores, he hurried into the kitchen to ask her a question.

"Mom, do you think I'm still a good person?"

"What kind of question is that one Andréu? After all the many trial that this family has been subjected to and that we thought we would never overcome, it was your contagious optimism that helped us to make all our lives more bearable. It doesn't matter what has happened in the country of the dollars, what you were and what you are still will forever be kept in the memory of all of us."
"Did you know that Ivan and Sarita are dating and have plans to get married?"
"Of course I know. What kind of mother would I be if I didn't know these things?"

Andreu commenced his monologue.

"That day at the airport, both of them were very nervous. They confessed their love to me, and I felt it was so beautiful. Such pure love can only bear fruits, but I also felt shame when they asked me for my blessing. The truth is that I lack the morality to judge anyone. Back in New York, I let myself go with an uncontrollable passion for an older woman. A woman who seduced all the men who crossed her way. I was driven by a bestial attraction, and did things with her that I shall take to my grave. I went against my own morals, my principles and everything that I have always believed in. But the saddest thing of all is knowing that I have no regrets about it and if I had the opportunity to be with her again, I would do it again without hesitation. Now Mama Socorro, now that you know the truth, do you still consider me a good man?"

Socorro left the kitchen for her bedroom, and after a few minutes rummaging in her old wardrobe she retrieved a rectangular jewel box. Opening up the box she said to Andreu "These letters were written back in 1989." Heaving a deep sigh, Socorro passed the wad of letters to her son.

"I have kept these letters for a long time, but not long enough to erase the memory of a man who I was so deeply in love with. I can assure you that by the time you finish reading them, you will find the peace you need." Socorro broke down and left the room with a lump in her throat and eyes wet with tears.

Andreu gently examined the written memories of his mother embodied in the seven letters. He put them in order by date and started to walk along his mother's past, the past she had just left in his hands. The first page was addressed at a young Socorro and the sender's name was John.

41
Hot dog stink

Having murdered Mary Smith and robbed her apartment, Hotdog Man loped through the streets of New York for a good hour, buoyed up by two supreme feelings: the first being an erotic happiness, and the second, and most important the painful impatience. "What am I going to do now with $ 5,000 and all the jewelry I have stolen?" Those jewels were worth a fortune. He could retire and live carefree for the rest of his life. So he locked himself in his apartment to reflect, and look for the answers to his questions. He would start a new life, a fresh start somewhere far, far away.

On Monday September 15, 2014, Mr. Aldo Rocamora found the body of Mary Smith on the marble floor of the living room, her head haloed in a sticky puddle of blood. He immediately called 911 and at two minutes past six in the morning, less than a quarter of an hour after he called the crime in; police, forensic examiners and other strangers surrounded the lifeless body.

The initial examination of the body revealed that she had been dead for about 24 hours, since rigor mortis had reached its maximum intensity. Mary Smith's corneal layers had shriveled to form a yellowish plaque, dry, hard, thick, with the same consistency as papyrus. It was also clear that a single sharp blow to her head, after which she bled to death, had caused her demise.

The question as to who had murdered Mary Smith was never resolved and would become yet another of the New York City Police Department's historic unsolved crimes. The only two people who knew the secret code for Mary Smith's private elevator were Mary herself and her butler, Aldo Rocamora. Rocamora had a perfect alibi. At the very moment that Mary was bleeding to death, Aldo was celebrating the wedding of his eldest daughter, Dorothy, in the state of Pennsylvania.

All three of her ex-husbands had alibis, and it would have been impossible for any of them to have killed Mary Smith. Margaret, perhaps the greatest beneficiary of Mary's will, was also in Pennsylvania, as Aldo's guest at Dorothy's wedding.

Crime scene investigators found no suspect fingerprints or traces of DNA from, anyone other than Rocamora or Mary herself. Nothing. Her phone records revealed that before she died, she had received a phone call from Cuba that further enquiries revealed it to be from Andreu Santa Rosa. In conclusion, Mary Smith's crime went unpunished. Strangely nobody noticed the smell of hot dogs that was diffused throughout the apartment like a languid and anemic spirit, hoping to tell everyone without any success – just who her exiled executioner had been.

42

The Testament of Mary Smith

When, on Saturday September 13, Andreu had told Mary that he loved her, he had lied, but not completely, because in all lies there are always some elements of truth. Of course he didn't love her in the same way that he loved Fernanda, but love is not a question of quantity but quality. He loved Mary differently. And it was a kind of love that was difficult for him to describe. In fact, it had hurt him to hear those final groans imagining that she was in the hands of another man, bringing her to one of her violent multiple orgasms. He didn't realize that Mary Smith had actually been murdered.

Mary Smith, one of the wealthiest and most powerful women in America and indeed the world, had died and we must emphasize that she had not perished or "kicked the bucket" she had just died. Despite all the success of professional life and all her money, just like an ordinary human being, she had been born alone and now she had died alone.

Her private funeral service was attended by her three former husbands, Margaret from her office and Mr. Rocamora, no more no less, and none of them lost their composure or wept for her. The five impassive faces revealed only consideration and respect. Nothing else.

The ceremony took place at a private crematorium. After the indignity of the autopsy it was as if the ignition of the fire was intended to warm up the ice woman she had been when she was alive and then later on the mortuary slab. Her ashes were handed to her former butler in a simple gold rectangular box.

And later at Mary's wake as Rocamora grimly stared at that little golden ark he thought to himself:

"Tell me now the use of your diets and the reasons for your rigorous daily exercise, now that you are just dust. "

Then he dismissed his thoughts and settled his exhausted body into a chair. He helped himself to some canapés from the servants circulating with trays, although it seemed strange for someone to serve him since he was no longer a butler or waiter.

Mr. Rocamora had inherited $ 10 million from the lady's estate. By testamentary disposition, the Miss MS publishing house and other businesses passed entirely to Margaret, who truly upset about the death of her goddess, promised to continue with her legacy.

The three former husbands didn't inherit anything. A few millions went to various charities and ten million dollars were destined to find way into a bank account for a Mr. Andreu Santa Rosa pending Mary's lawyer discovering his whereabouts.

Just before Andreu had decided to return to Cuba, Mary Smith had instructed her lawyers to change her will so that both Andreu and Mr. Aldo Rocamora bagged the same 10 million dollar windfall, since both in Mary Smith's opinion had provided her with "excellent services".

The testament of Mary Smith was written with impressive clarity of thought proving once again who Mary was in life: a woman of few, but great ideas, which she examined regularly and applied perfectly, right up to her last testament.

As the coffin slid into the flames, the chosen song to celebrate her life was Meat Loaf's Dead Ringer For Love. Nobody at the funeral service thought it was distasteful.

43
The bet

1989, Havana, Cuba

Twenty five years ago, before Andreu, Johan or Patrick had been born Mary Smith was 23 years old and Johan's father John was 26, like his friend Richard Milton.

They had decided to take a vacation to Cuba. It is true that back in 1989 there was no United States embassy on the island, because America had no diplomatic relations with Cuba, but tours to the Cuban tourist paradise for Americans had begun years before then, even though it meant taking a detour via Mexico or Canada.

By then the young John was already a compulsive gambler, one of those gamblers with fixed and disrespectful eyes, quite capable of gambling it all away in the big casinos. And so, John and his friend Richard Milton, the future first husband of Mary Smith, arrived at the big hotels of Havana. As they moved from the Commodore to the Copacabana, they discovered the top quality gambling to be had and John remarked about how true it was when people said that "there were no hotels in Cuba only casinos with accommodation and other 'services'.

Neither one of them spoke good enough Spanish to get by, but they found Federico the interpreter, who was apparently a 55-year-old retired military man from Bayamo. Federico was married, but he lived with his lover, Doña Catita.

****

That night John and Richard took Federico to the biggest casino in Havana, The Havana Club Casino. It was off limits to Cuban nationals, but open to any foreigner with enough money. From 1989, Cuba would welcome 326,300 visitors and 204 million dollars would come with them. The tourism sector had become the main driving motor of the Cuban economy.

First they went to the roulette table, but following heavy losses, Richard realized he had got a sudden headache and decided not to play any more. John, however, was agitated, mad and in a panic, he rushed over to the poker table because he was convinced that this was the night he was going to win big.

John was ready to play and win a mountain of gold. He was enthralled with the extraordinary splendor of the Cuban casino, without having a care about losing the vast sums of money that he then could afford.

John was a gambler, drinker, smoker and womanizer. For him it was an inevitable affair. John was always chasing the same goal: winning or taking something from others and in his game everything was possible, especially women.

He spent the whole night at the casino and after he had lost every penny he had, a new bet turned up. Possessed by the demon of his passion and his unlimited greed, John listened carefully as the new game was explained.

"You have lost everything Mr. John." The winner, who was a presumptuous Russian by the name Matei, admonished John. "But we are all gentlemen in here and

I propose another game." As Federico translated Matei's Spanish, John found himself paying full attention to the Russian. "There is a beautiful girl in Bayamo whose name is Socorro. It is said that her beauty is so extraordinary that men travel from all over Cuba just to see her. " Federico readily confirmed himself that everything Matei was saying was true.

"I can confirm that everything Mr. Matei has said is true, she is a splendid woman." Federico added and John continued to listen to the story that unfolded

"The girl is a virgin and I give you a month to get her." Matei explained as John mentally scored this new bet. "If you can deflower her within a month, I will pay you back in full all the money that you have lost tonight. And if you don't deflower her, then you will have to double my winning." The Russian concluded his offer.

"All right." John answered gravely.

Richard was disgusted with the pair of them.

"This is a dirty game." Richard lectured his friend once they left the casino. "This goes right against my moral convictions. It's one thing to play with money, but a very different thing to play with a human being and in this case a women." Richard continued the scolding as they walked back to their hotel, but John just ignored him.

"Federico." John sang. "Take me to Bayamo right now."

44
The Young Mary Smith

While John and Richard were living it up in Cuba, the young Mary Smith was only 23 years old. Her parents had provided her with the finest of educations, from governesses and private tutors during her childhood and adolescence, to the very best private schools. In 1989 Mary Smith graduated with honors, the first in her year in Linguistics and English Literature at New York's Columbia University - the most expensive college in America.

Her parents (who were both to be killed in a car accident two years later) had only ever felt responsible for the academic upbringing of their daughter, but had never trained in her love. Therefore Mary knew of courtesies and books, but nothing of affection.

During her Columbia University years, Mary fell in love with a young boy of a different social rank; he was one of the university waiters. Mary didn't care about that because she was truly and crazily in love with him.

They had become good friends, and she could not help but love him a little bit more every day, savoring his green eyes, where she could often see herself reflected in his pupils, as she enjoyed some delightful thoughts. However, Mary could not understand why this young boy after talking with her for four long years had never taken the first step to stroke her hand or steal a kiss.

Mary Smith loved him and she loved him with all her heart. And since she had never loved anyone before she was willing to wait for as long as necessary. She even thought that he might be homosexual, but she did not care because she loved him a lot. Mary knew the correct verb was "love" because she just wanted to be with him at any hour of the day; inventing excuses to spend more time with him in the university restaurant where he worked and when they talked, her whole body shuddered with excitement.

So on the day of her graduation, Mary decided to present him with her virginity. She invited him back to her luxurious residence flat; the one that cost Mary's parents $ 30,000 annually. Mary smiled as he approached her to plant his full lips on her mouth for a long velvety kiss. She knew then with certainty that he was not gay and that he liked women.

At the time Mary was so inexperienced that to offer him her virginity, was she considered the best of all her gifts, but she was also very scared and did not know what to do. He was more experienced and concealed within his jacket was a cheap bottle of whiskey. Mary was ready for everything, absolutely everything. It was her graduation day and she was going to celebrate with the man she loved.

But he used her inexperience to exact a cruel revenge. Once the cheap whisky had done its job, he thrust into her unceremoniously with not a shred of affection Oh yes, she ended up paying for the complexes given to the boy who lunged inside her, punishing her because she was a rich girl and he was only a waiter. He had been the slave of rich daddy's boys and girls for four long years and she was going to pay for that. He fucked her as many times as he could, taking her vagina, he mouth and her anus, while she was deliriously bleeding. When he had finished, he kissed her cheek and offered her a very cordial handshake. She shook his hand coldly, but deep inside Mary wanted revenge. He was the one who one day would pay her back.

****

And for all these reasons, five years later, when Mary Smith turned 28 and opened her own publishing house, she saw the need to employ a butler to cater for her needs.

She visited the most renowned agency in New York and inspected all the butlers on their register one by one, but when she glimpsed those green eyes, she knew she had to choose him: Mr. Aldo Rocamora.

Once the two of them were alone in the interview room Mary expressed her newfound dominance.

"You will gather all my crap. You will clean all my shit. You will only receive my filth and my trash. You will be my slave until the end of my days. "

Mr. Aldo Rocamora accepted his fate, lowered his head and whispered the thrilling words: "I hope that one day you will forgive me."

45
A second in time

John had taken the bet very seriously. Cold blooded and insolent he started to plot how he was going to deflower the young woman. He was a gambler and the bet was an exciting challenge. He was constantly asking about that girl, whom did she know and what were her hobbies. Federico deliberately tried to evade the answers because he could sniff the future scandal, but a few more dollars convinced him to respond at length.

"She is a good girl. She likes music and dancing like any other Cuban girl." Federico replied with a sigh.
"Music and dance?" John thought to himself. "Perfect. Let's give the Cubanita the two."

(First Letter)

Dear John:

Yesterday I had a wonderful time with you. It is such a long time since I have been so amused. As you can see I am fascinated by dance and music, although I have noticed that it is not your forte.

I know that this will not last forever. You're only here for a business commitment and while you are here in Cuba for a month or two, hopefully in that time we will get to know each other better, and become good friends.

Believe it or not, here the boys of my age group are still very immature and only think about sleeping around with anyone they meet, but you're so different.

You know I could spend so many long hours listening to all your stories and I would never get tired.

Well I must say good-bye for now, wishing that you thought of me as much as I think of you.

Your friend Socorro Santa Rosa

****

Andreu stopped reading the letter to do a little math subtraction. If Mama Socorro was 41 years old and had been born in 1972, then when she wrote this letter his mother must have been at the innocent age of 17 years. He was well aware of the legendary beauty of his mother. Many people talked about it, particularly Doña Catita who always made him blush. She was always saying that he was very handsome and it was all thanks to his mother's genes since he had taken nothing from his father. His green eyes, well no one knew where they had come from because no one else in the family had them.

"Tell me more about my mother, Doña Catita." Andreu begged every time Catalina started talking about his mother.
"Andreu, oh your mother was a very beautiful girl, her smile could bring ten men to hover over her." Catalina let go with that peculiar cackle that older people have, and then clearing her throat with an almighty cough continued her story.

46
A second in time (continuation)

"Men of all ages from all over Cuba went to surrender at the feet of your mother, after countless efforts, they always returned to their homes with the disappointment of having failed to woo the beautiful Socorro." Dona Catita explained.

Andreu paused his memories to gather his thoughts.

If his mother was such a beautiful woman as Dona Catita said, how was it possible that she finished up in the arms of Gerardo Montiel, an evil man, a consummate alcoholic, who hid in his vice the cowardly desire, to physically and emotionally abuse her?

When Andreu was old enough to confront his father, he had done so with all his might. His drunken father continually subjecting his mother to beatings whenever Socorro didn't have a bottle of rum ready for him or his dinner was cold. Any excuse had been good enough for Gerardo to beat her up.

This last time it happened, Socorro had made a serious mistake, believing that her husband was unconscious because he had drunk too much, she thought it would be safer to escape with the children and take shelter at a friend's house. But as she gathered Sarita and Jasmine in her arms, each only 9 and 5 years old, she could not have foreseen that that lump that was lying on the sofa would grab her hair - without even caring about the welfare of the children that were in her arms.

Gerardo pulled at her hair while desperately Socorro, called for the teenage Andreu to take the children that she was carrying in her arms and take them off to safety.

First Andreu pulled his younger brother off his mother's leg and then he grabbed Sarita and Jasmine in one fluid motion. He turned the doorknob and running with all his strength in his legs took his brothers and sister to Dona Catita's house, several blocks away. His younger siblings safe Andreu returned to the house where his mother was under attack.

With copious tears stinging his eyes and heart pounding he had run back home, overtaken by the terrible fear of a son who was scared for his mother's life.

As he entered the house his body froze when he saw his father's hands dripping blood onto the floor, the product of the violent beating he had just applied to Andreu's mother's face. It was then that those innocent tears stopped, and instead Andreu was possessed by an uncontrollable rage that drove him to punch and kick his father, and he didn't stop until he was sure his mother was out of danger.

Gerardo ran away after the beating with a sneer, but not before threatening Andreu for interfering in his matters and revealing for the first time the astonishing secret: "you are not my son, you are the unwanted child of a foreigner."

Those words hurt Socorro more deeply in her heart than any of Gerardo's punches had
Andreu tried to suppress that painful memory from his mind, but he felt a metallic taste in his mouth. "How hard life had been for his mother Socorro." He thought to himself. And still he couldn't understand why she had decided to stay with a man who only hurt her for so long.

Andreu decided to continue reading the letters, but first he paused to drink a good slug of tequila – from the bottle that he kept in his bedroom and the fiery spirit helped him to cope with the guilt in his heart. His heart divided between two women, the passion he felt for Mary, which was taking him to the brink of losing Fernanda.

47
Full Moon
(Second letter)

Dear John,

I still can't believe it. After a week of dating you, a true gentleman, I feel this attraction towards you so strongly, and although I was dying to try the taste of your mouth, the truth is that I just couldn't dare to be the first one to take that step.

It was in the "Malecón de Copacabana", after having that dinner with you, the one that Russian friend of yours, Matei, so generously offered to pay for, that you took my hand and we both headed out for a walk. United by our hands, sweet images rolled through my head of a new world filled of love with you, thoughts that to me were before unknown.

And while my mind wandered, you had the courage to take me gently by the neck and give me the tender kiss I had ever have dreamed of, and the glowing full moon was the only witness of that, my first kiss, a moment I will always treasure forever.

I don't know what you are doing to me, John but I can't stop thinking of you.
I love you.

Socorro.

****

Andreu felt some little relief on discovering that not everything in the life of his mother had been a tribulation. Andreu was delighted when she revealed in the letter that at some point in her life she had got to know happiness and then a mutual love. With all his strength Andreu wished he were like John and be able to go off with Fernanda and do all those nice things that this good man had done for his mother. But Andreu knew he couldn't run to Fernanda and apologize, let alone write to her with a symbolic kiss as a sign of his apology. In Andreu's opinion, that couldn't happen because that only happened in stories about fairy princesses. So he dropped this crazy idea from his mind and spent the rest of the night reading the letters of the young Mama Socorro.

*****

There was a knock at the front door. It was eleven o'clock at night and everyone in the house was sleeping, Andreu got up and left his room to go and see who it was. A man, indeed a stranger by his appearance, breathing heavily while trying to unknot his tie and undo the top button of his shirt, unable to bear the Cuban heat. His hair and beard were red, irrefutable proof of his foreign origin.

"Are you Mr. Andreu Santa Rosa? "He gasped breathlessly before adding. "May I come in?" Andreu only nodded back to him. "Okay. Nice to meet you. I am Mary Smith's lawyer." He explained as he shook Andreu's hand.
"What?" Andreu asked, unable to hide his astonishment that Mary's lawyer should have followed him to Cuba.
"I am going to have explain myself better." The foreigner continued, this time in perfect unaccented Spanish. "I repeat that I am Mary Smith's lawyer. My name is Karl Pont and I understand that you were closely linked to Mary Smith because you have just inherited 10 million dollars from her."

Andreu hesitated momentarily as what Pont had just told him sunk in, then invited him to enter the house. After offering the lawyer a cold glass of water, Andreu joined him on the couch.

"I do not understand how I have inherited $ 10 million." Andreu was clearly confused by what Pont had just told him.

"Miss Mary Smith died on September 13, 2014. She was murdered."

It was with that last part of Pont's statement that Andreu realized that everything was not some kind of joke.

"She was murdered." Andréu muttered clearly stunned by the revelation.

"That is correct and the murder was violent too." Karl said with a very human smile. "She was struck on the head while she was talking on the telephone, we believe to you. The phone company records showed that yours was the last phone call that she received on that final Saturday of her life. The police think that your voice must have been the last thing she heard before she died." Karl examined Andreu's reaction as he spoke.

"And, you haven't found the murderer?" Andreu asked softly.

"No." Karl reddened. "But I must fulfill my duty." He added as he retrieved a folder from his briefcase. "If you want the ten million you must sign these papers and let me know the bank account number where we can transfer the money to you."

"I do not know what to say." Andreu answered feeling the nausea building in his throat.

"You don't have to say anything. It was Mary's last wish to give you the money, so sign here, if you please." Karl repeated offering Andreu his gold Mountblanc fountain pen to sign the documents.

Mary Smith was well aware that anyone who comes into conspicuous wealth in Cuba could fall foul of the Marxist government's philosophy so in her will she left instructions that the ten million dollars Andreu was due to inherit would be paid into a Swiss bank, from, which Andreu could gradually transfer small amounts to his bank account in Cuba. And so in this manner, Andreu became a rich Cuban. However, he would never show off about his riches to anyone. When he was asked about where the money came from for the new air conditioning that he had installed, or why he didn't need to switch the lights off to save energy, Andreu answered that the money came from an American insurance policy that he took out when he worked for Miss MS Publishing.

Over time, Andreu didn't become ostentatious. He didn't waste his money for pleasure or squander it on useless things. And while it was true that occasionally he would take himself along to some expensive Spanish restaurant Havana, he didn't lead a lavish lifestyle. In this way he didn't cause envy in others and simply played by the rules of the Cuban game. From the moment he inherited the 10 million dollars, he never lacked anything, but his future, my dear readers, like the future of Carmen Spain and Orlando The Great - is another story ... another long story.

48
Culpability

However, we must now return to the present and take note that Andreu had received the devastating news of Mary Smith's death. The saddest thing was knowing that the time he had spoken to her for the very last time, the time when he imagined that she was reaching climatic orgasms with another man, she was in fact dying. Her last groan had been her final sigh of life. He felt like dying himself as he remembered the voice of that woman of steel imploring him with her last breath to say, "I love you" with the sweetness of his voice.

"Tell me something nice.," the dying Mary Smith had begged as she was mortally wounded.

Raging with impotence, Andreu threw everything he could lay his hands on in the apartment against the walls. All the members of his family were now awake and watching him without understanding why he was doing it or how to react. It was the first time for all of them that they had seen the face of Andreu contorted with utter desolation.

It was Mama Socorro, who could feel the terrible pain of her son within herself, who sent everybody back to his or her respective rooms so that she could attempt to calm Andreu down. Socorro did everything possible to comfort her son, who was beyond listening to anything he was being told. Andreu's heart was broken and even the love of his mother didn't have the strength to heal his broken organ.

For days he wandered - insensibly – through and about the streets of his beloved Bayamo, dragging himself along with his battered heart. Uninterested in his appearance it deteriorated rapidly, even with the ten million-dollars Andreu was unable to recover. In the streets he ate like a beggar, eating what he found or what kindly people gave to him. At night he slept in abandoned and dark streets.

"How could he bear the grief of knowing that the woman he so much admired, that he loved so much, was now dead? That woman who lacked so much love from anyone else and that only he tried to give her, was now dead.

"Damn you Mary Smith." He shouted again and again with his breath stinking of cheap rum. "Why the hell didn't you tell me that there was someone in your apartment? Why didn't you take advantage of those precious minutes you had to call the police or your security, instead of just wanting to hear my voice tell you that I loved you? Why are you forcing me to carry this guilt?"

With a sudden movement he smashed the rum bottle he had been trying to assuage his guilt with against the wall and inadvertently cut his right hand with the broken neck of the bottle. The sharp glass suggested to him silently, the sadistic idea of suicide. In his confused state Andreu held the razor sharp glass to his carotid. A trickle of warm blood rolled down his neck to join the sweat and tears staining his shirt. He stood for a few seconds thinking, waiting for his mind to give him that final command to push and end his miserable existence.

Like any student of medicine, he knew perfectly well that the final thrust would be clean and lethal.

Like a ray of hopeful light, the words of Mom Socorro soaked into his deranged reasoning.

"I assure you Andreu that by the time you finish reading these letters you will feel much better."

Then he remembered that a few days ago, when Mary Smith's lawyer had knocked at his door he had quickly gathered his mother's letters together and stuffed them into his pockets.

Desperately he sought for that last vestige of his mother, and although the letters were badly damaged they were still readable.

49
A strange feeling
(Third letter)

Hello my Dear John,

I was confused by your reaction last night when I tried to invite you back to my house for you to get to know my parents. I noticed that the grin on your countenance was replaced with a grimace. But I also know that your words were not meaningless. I understand that it was not yet the right time to meet my family, and that I shouldn't have put that pressure on you.

You're always so solid with your arguments; I am convinced that it is worthy to prolong the waiting until we can prove that our relationship is definitely serious.

I'll be frank. The answer you gave me, I didn't like it at first and perhaps this is to do with my age and my youth, because I want to scream to the world that you and I are dating. Anyway I will be patient. Nobody in my family knows that we are going out together, but the truth is that I am finding it harder to find excuses to run into your arms.

I can assure you that nothing will stop me from seeing you tomorrow. Your last comment left me intrigued: "Dear Socorro." (You told me.) "You know that these days have been wonderful for me and I never thought that in such a short period of time I could end up falling in love with as lovely a girl as you. I don't know what you've done to me but I am in love with you. I hope that next time we meet, you will let me show you how much I love you. "

My Dear John, I've got everything ready for tomorrow. I will escape on the pretext of going to visit Catalina who has fallen a little sick these days. I am very excited about seeing you again and I know I will find it very difficult to sleep tonight.

Forever Yours

Socorro.

On that night 25 years ago, Socorro's joy helped Andreu to finally sleep peacefully again.

50
Love Between The Lines (first part)

And while Socorro's love story occurred in the past, the love of Fernanda seemed to volatilize in the present. Andreu was consumed by drink and Mary Smith was dust in a golden box. The world continued spinning between love and lack of love because life goes on jumping from love to hate ... love and hate, and this goes on forever. And here we are, all of us with our personal stories which are merely copies of previous stories and will once more be played out in the future by somebody else; in this way we all are the plagiarism stocks of yesterday and tomorrow.

And in this present that we all share with our friends and enemies, love and lack of love, Orlando The Great, the famous writer of Mexican Love, had read in Hello Magazine that Mary Smith had been murdered. How much he had admired that woman, even with their differences! Once he met her in person, he immediately fell in love with her. Orlando hesitated as to whether he should shed a few little tears because he considered her murder not only like a life lost, but also almost a sacrilege, but following the inspiration that took him at that moment he wept for that great woman who had left this world with a final sigh. And since he had given his word to Mary Smith that he would contact Carmen Spain, he did, because a true promise continues even after death. He decided to talk to her over the Internet and typed Carmenspain@ntlworld.com into his e-mail address box.

"Hi. I am Orlando The Great. Do you know who I am?" Orlando was satisfied with what he had written. Only a minute passed before he received a response from Carmen.

"Don't you know yourself who you are, why do you have to ask me?"

Her reply brought a smile to Orlando's face and he reread her message three times. This Carmen was definitely a mordacious woman.

"Have a beautiful day." Orlando answered.
"Thanks and the same to you." She replied and from this he deduced that she was a direct woman.
"I will try." Orlando typed back.
"You will try, what?" With this third response he derived that in addition to directness, she was also a fierce woman.
"I will try to have a beautiful day, but my failures are also extraordinary. We, writers, are like this. I send you a kiss." Orlando typed as he started to enjoy their little game.
"My failures are also extraordinary and I am not a writer." She replied quickly. "And please do not send me kisses."

Irritated by this latest response Orlando began to lose his temper.

"All right. Can I see you? It's a promise I made to the late Mary Smith. I am here in Spain right now on a promotional tour for my latest novel Mexican Love. Orlando clicked send, but five minutes went by and Carmen did not answer. "Are you there? Can I see you or not?" he typed furiously

"I am sorry." She replied.

"Well, my little magical elf, when can I can see you then?" He typed in a more relaxed frame of mind.

"I need an answer from you right now." She typed back.

"Why have you called me a "magical elf"? It is very important to me that you tell me."

"For me an elf is a being who appears to us suddenly and brings us magic. One day I'd like to see some of your written work. I imagine it would Kafkaesque." He replied cautiously.

"You haven't made a single mistake in anything you have written to me." She fired back quickly. "You don't forget to use capital letters in the right places either. You are trying to psychoanalyze me and I do not like it when people try to psychoanalyze me. I don't write well. Kafka was a genius and I am just mediocre. You're irritating me. Your statement "we, writers" in plural, shows your need to feel supported by others, or to belong to a group; it exposes your insecurities and fears. What's wrong with you Orlando?"

Orlando was outraged by her latest tirade and it took him several deep breaths to calm himself and reply sarcastically:

"Shall we meet then so that we can continue our interesting conversation? Kisses." He added, "kisses" just to annoy her.
"I told you not to send me kisses." She typed back clearly irritated by his ploy. "And why do you need us to meet in order to continue our conversation? Are you so bored on your own?"
"I'd like you to be able to form the correct opinion of my person." He typed without thinking because Carmen was now really getting on his nerves.
"I do not need to see you to form the correct opinion of you." She replied adding more fuel to the fire. "What is so important about my opinion of the great Orlando?"
"I care about what each human being thinks about me, but I am always more interested in the opinions of people as rare as you." He added.
"Well you shouldn't care. My opinions are not worth a shit."

"If you had the correct opinion of me, you wouldn't have supposed that I'm bored or that I would want to see you out of boredom. Boredom has never happened in my life."

"Thanks for everything Orlando The Great. I am not interested in getting to know you."

"Damned Spaniard." Orlando swore to himself. "She is vain and conceited and petulant ... I'm sure she is uglier than a cockatoo."

"Damned Mexican." Carmen exclaimed to herself. "He thinks he is smart ass, chauvinist, giving himself airs and graces."

****

Their curiosity piqued both of them started to browse the Internet in order to spy on one another. Were they on Facebook, Twitter, YouTube or LinkedIn? Were there any photos online? Was Carmen an ugly, sexually frustrated, obese hag? Was Orlando a grotesque monster? They spent hours prying into each other's lives.

51
Test of Love
(Fourth Letter)

My beloved John,

If my past letters confirmed a true friendship between us, this has now changed and now after the consummation of our love, my feeling of giving myself to you in every sense has transformed our relationship. It is now also clear to me that when you leave Cuba, all of the letters that I have written to you, that are in your beautiful hands will be my final gift, or rather a reminder of the firm promise that you have made to me that you will come back to me, once you have bought that house in the United States, where we can live together for the rest of our lives.

For a moment I hesitated to offer you my virginity, but seeing the blue of your eyes, I realized that the words from your mouth were bathed in the sincerest of truths. It was then that all my doubts evaporated completely and I gave you the last vestige of my person which still belonged only to myself, and that now is yours. It was the sign of chastity that kept my innocent body for you.

Other than that now you own me. You have taken possession of my body and of my thoughts. From the moment my eyes glance the first rays of dawn I think only of you.

And I confess that I spend hours in front of the mirror, trying to capture a pose or the appropriate smile for you to love me, but it is I who when you smile, am the one who ends up falling in love with you a little bit more every day.

I hope with all my heart that all the words that you promised me yesterday soon become a sweet reality.

Forever Yours
Socorro

****

It was unusually cold that day in tropical Cuba, but Andreu felt warmer after reading his mother's beautiful narrative, she undoubtedly knew him better than she knew the back of her own hand. She had already predicted that by the time he had finished reading her memoirs, his heart would be in harmony. "How wise my mom is." And it was true because now Andreu had put his suicidal intentions behind him. His mind was clear, he would return home as soon he finished reading the remaining three letters.

****

Twenty five years back in time when the young Socorro was only 17 years old she looked at herself in her bedroom mirror and realized that she was in trouble. The shooting pains in her innocent belly suddenly worsened and she tried to calm down this magical pain, a mix of suffering and joy, with the sweet memory of having offered John the most intimate corner of her carnal flesh. She thought that perhaps others might notice her changes. "Could people guess that she was no longer the same woman? Was it possible that they had discovered that she had transmuted?" Doña Catita had told her that her face was shining. "Does a woman after being deflowered sparkle differently?"

****

John felt nothing. The emotion of guilt wasn't in his vocabulary and his face showed only an icy passionless indifference. Before returning to the United States he had already talked to Matei and collected on his bet.

"I won." Exclaimed John as Matei stood still with his mouth wide open in amazement.

"You deflowered her?" The Russian was surprised.

"I deflowered her." John confirmed and Matei laughed cheekily.

"Damn." Said the Russian wiping away his tears of laughter. "That is the most expensive hymen in my life. 10,000 dollars for a fucking hymen. All right." Matei complained. "You can leave now. Our debt is settled."

52
My sad truth
(Fifth Letter)

My adored John,

I am writing to you because it is all I can do to stem my urge to yell at the world that our love blossoms and grows stronger every day, like an orchid that has endured the hard winter season.

I'm now in my room and after having fulfilled all my chores, I do nothing but walk around and around in circles, looking for the right time to tell my parents that we are committed to marry. I want to prepare the grounds for you so that you are welcomed perfectly here.

First I want to let them know that you're a wonderful man. You are hard working and a man unlike any others who is willing to ask for my hand with all the formality that the situation requires, and that we will get married when you return to my beloved Cuba with a traditional seaside wedding ceremony; once you have solved your problems in the United States and have bought the house where over time we will see our children grow up.

Of course the wedding date is yet to set, but I am quite sure that the moment you come to ask for my hand, my family will accept our compromise and that they will give us all their unconditional support.

I've studied everything very well and have come to the conclusion that it shall be tonight during dinner that I will tell them all about us.

Wish me all the luck and with a little bit of fortune today I will be giving you some very good news in my next letter.

****

And as she had planned in her letter, Socorro waited for her parents to be seated comfortably the dining room before she spoke to them. After a hard day at work, and having eaten his dinner, her father was relaxing in his big chair, exhaling the heavy smoke from his thick Cuban cigar.

Meanwhile, her loving and caring mother, just as she did every evening, had taken to her knitting basket to do her crochet, which helped to release her stress.

After a long and deep breath, Socorro stood up in front of her parents to tell them the story of her furtive love.

"Mom, Dad, I want to ask ... well ... tell you really ... that I have had a boyfriend for almost two weeks now, and we love each other and I'd like you to meet him."

Then the fragile Socorro took a pause to identify any reaction on the faces of her parents that would indicate to her what to say next. It was her father who uttered the first words.

"I am not going to lie to you, Soco." Soco was the diminutive name he used to affectionately call her. "The truth is that I am not very happy because you are not yet 18 years old and we already have a suitable boyfriend for you at the door of our house. You have always been known as a very decent girl who has always done the correct thing. I am finding it very difficult to accept that you are no longer the little girl I used to carry in my arms when taking her to sleep in her room. In addition to being as beautiful as you are, which of course is all thanks to me ... "Her father laughed a little to make it clear to his child that she still had his full support in all matters and to dissipate some of the momentary tension. "I have always been well aware of all your suitors and among them I hope you have chosen the right one."

Socorro's mum was very happy to listen to the words of her husband, which denoted his great maturity, and wisdom and so she decided to join the conversation.

"Tell us Soco, who's the lucky guy? Is he from here from Bayamo? Do we know him? Come on girl. Tell us who he is."

It was then that Socorro realized how difficult it was going to be to explain the rest of her story, because although her parents had already accepted that their daughter had a boyfriend, they were still unaware that he was a foreigner.

"No mummy. He is not from Bayamo, or any other nearby city. Moreover, he is not even Cuban."

The eyes of his father narrowed as if trying to decipher what Socorro was saying.

"What do you mean he is not from Cuba? So where is he from? Socorro please explain what this is all about? Are you playing a cruel joke to us?"

Meanwhile her mother's vocal cords were paralyzed, she just stood still with her mouth open and her hands glued to her face.

"Well. He is a young American boy, who came to Cuba on a business trip, but I can assure you that he is an honest man and he doesn't want me to just be his girlfriend. He wants to come here and talk to you so that he can ask you for my hand."
"But, what are you talking about Socorro? Have you gone mad? You don't even know him and you are already speaking of marriage?" Her father rebuked her.

"No father. You are wrong. I assure you that he is a good man and if you allow me I will go to his hotel, which is here on the coast, to confirm with him everything I have told you. Please, for heaven's sake have confidence in me. I will not let you down."

After nodding their heads in agreement Socorro went off in search of John and she felt very unlucky when she arrived at his hotel only to find he wasn't there.

It was an old and still persistent suitor of Socorro, Gerardo Montiel, who immediately indicated to the beautiful girl where she would find her lover. She thanked him with a faint smile, not realizing what that traitor had prepared for her.

53
The Cliff
(Sixth letter)

I ran with all my strength, my love, and I was so pleased to see you with your beautiful blonde hair at the entrance of the casino talking to your Russian friend, Matei.

I walked slowly towards you to give you the big news, but then a shift in my heart stopped me abruptly.

"So tell me, my good friend John, how did you manage to steal Socorro's virginity? Tell me everything if you want your debt to be cancelled." Matei demanded with sheer malice, as he could see Socorro trembling with fear behind John.

"It wasn't too difficult Matei. With provincial and uneducated women like Socorro you just need to know how to talk them, and be able to show them that you are a man of the world. From then on everything becomes so easy. So easy that the poor fool believes you blindly when you tell her you are going to marry her." He laughed as he said this and that seemed to please Matei no end. "If she had known, the stupid naïve girl, that I am already engaged to a lady – you know the real kind - Socorro would certainly have had a heart attack. Fortunately the only thing that was holding me here in this dump was my debt to you, and since I have now cleared that, I can leave for London on the first plane out of here." John paused for a moment puzzled as to what the Russian was finding so amusing, "What's up Matei? What are you finding so entertaining?" John turned to look behind him and beheld Socorro in floods of tears. At that point John understood that his cruel confession had been orchestrated by Matei in order to humiliate Socorro.

Such was John's contempt and lack of moral fiber that he merely finished off his whiskey and said.

"You deserved that for being so stupidly naïve." It was the last thing John ever said to her.

John's best friend, Richard Milton had watched the whole sorry scene unfold with disgust, and when Socorro ran off in tears, he went to find her scarred that she might commit suicide or harm herself. Chasing her through the streets of Bayamo he eventually overtook her and grabbed her arm to bring her to a halt. For his efforts Richard received a heavy slap to the face that left a livid purple bruise on his cheek. The cornered Socorro looked just like a wounded animal in a trap howling with pain.

Despite the pain Richard's nobility showed through once again when seeing her so helpless, he gathered her up in his arms and Socorro just collapsed into his embrace like a rag doll.

"I'm so sorry about what just happened." Richard whispered in a guilty tone. "What John has done to you is shameless, but I'm not here to excuse him. I am here to ask you for your forgiveness because it has been my silence that has aided John's villainy. I know it is now too late to do anything, but if you ever need my help do not hesitate to contact me. I'll do anything if you will forgive me."

Richard let go of her and turned his back since he was no longer able to confront her pained visage. Drawing his pocket book out from his jacket he turned back and offered Socorro a flawless opal card with his name and telephone number.

****

There are very few people in the world who keep their promises, but Richard Milton was one of them. It was he, who thanks to his diplomatic connections, managed to secure a permanent US visa for Andreu. And it was he who persuaded Mary Smith to give Andreu a job in her company.

John, Johan's father, knew about the existence of his illegitimate son from his brief liaison with Socorro because Richard had told him about Andreu and so when his legitimate son asked him to help his friend, John did not hesitate and offered him the New York apartment. At the end of the day, the years had sweetened his heart and Andreu was after all his son – even if he was the product of a bet that he had won a long time ago.

54
Love Between The Lines (second part)

When Andreu read the sixth letter, deep inside him one could hear his tormented heart being torn into pieces - pieces so tiny – that he knew it was impossible to put them back together again. And while his tears were so painful, the world carried on with its stories of love and lack of love and so too life went on.

While Andreu was shocked that at the hands of one ruthless man, his mother's heart had been buried somewhere in Bayamo, the world continued turning. People lived on with their repetitive stories of love over time and distance.

****

After analyzing all of his Internet research, Orlando The Great was pleased to discover that Carmen Spain was not as ugly as a cockatoo. She didn't have one leg shorter than the other either, or an eye patch covering an empty socket. Thanks to the photographs he had discovered on various news websites he realized that she was a very special woman who though she found it difficult to smile could occasionally burst out laughing with good grace. When she laughed, the expression on of her face lost its hard edge of seriousness. She seemed to be a sensible woman, but also a fighter who liked only to be surrounded by her old friends. She was neither especially pretty nor ugly, but could be said to be attractive. Her lips were full, pink and sensual and they seemed to beg him to eagerly devour them. She had beautiful eyes, but a slightly dangerous look, as if a mere glance was enough to forbid anyone to touch or kiss her. Orlando sat there looking at her contradictory countenance, with that mouth that was shouting to be kissed and the eyes as forbidding as the red light of the traffic signal. Her skin was white, almost blue (at least in the photographs). Her hair, fixed in a rigid ponytail, was brunette.

From the photographs that showed her full figure, Orlando imagined how he would like to see her completely naked, but he couldn't do it. He immediately considered it a rude thought; since he had always believed that stripping any woman of her clothes (even just with your thoughts) was a dirty affair if she didn't consensually agree to do it. The most beautiful thing in the world for Orlando was to admire a beautiful naked woman, but only with her consent.

One week following their last communication, after tracking down her address in Madrid, he sent her a bouquet of pink roses. Orlando then waited for a couple of days before sending her a follow up message. He was hoping that the beautiful flowers would somehow tame the lady.

"Did you get the roses?" Was Orlando's simple opening question.
"Yes." Was Carmen's blunt answer and nothing more.
"Did you like them?" He asked.
"No, I didn't." She replied.
"Why was that?" Orlando enquired.
"Because I do not like pink." She answered.
"Why?" He asked with renewed curiosity.
"Because pink is the feminine color par excellence, the stereotype of women's sweetness." She explained and Orlando could visualize her shrugging her shoulders.
"And I'm not sweet." She added.
"What color do you like then?" He typed into the keyboard eager to know what her answer would be.
"I don't want to tell you." She replied.
"I shall send you some black flowers then." He typed back sarcastically.
"Okay." She replied with feigned indifference.

They both smiled into the reflected light of their computer screens, because they were both enjoying their little game. She had also enquired into Orlando's life and discovered that he didn't have a squint. He didn't have thin legs, and a large and flabby belly. Behind his dark glasses, his eyes looked uneasy with their sweet matte hazelnut tone. His mouth was cute and his face gave the impression that, in his youth, he may have experienced the odd fling from time to time, but that he was now tired of having adventures with any beautiful woman. He now wanted to embark on a peaceful and serious relationship, which would offer no big surprises or shocks. He was now ready for a stable partner with whom he could share what was left of his life.

Carmen studied Orlando's photographs and writings and through them also tried to discover his soul. Carmen, however, could not stop herself from visualizing Orlando naked because that was what she did with any man she liked. That was Carmen's curse to undress the men who had inflamed her imagination and that included Orlando The Great. So she passed him through her mental X-ray. He was in his forties - like her. He had broad chest and shoulders and big arms, probably from playing tennis or some other ball sport. She could work this out because of the hypertrophy of his right arm, which was more developed than the left, and as she continued with the cerebral radiography she decided that she wanted to meet him.

****

Two days after Orlando had sent the red roses he typed out his next message.

"Did you receive the flowers?"
"Yes."
"Did you like them?"
"Yes."
"Why?"
"Because they are red."
"Okay."

They each sat still not knowing what next to write.

"It would be very nice to meet you." She typed without a second thought.
"We could become good friends and colleagues." He typed back delighted at the prospect of meeting her.

55
Some Wise Advice

With the feeling that all of his energy had abandoned him, a bitter Andreu headed back to his family home to find out once and for all, how Mama Socorro could help him to climb out of this misery. In a way, his mother's letters reaffirmed his own belief that, just as John didn't deserve Socorro's love, he was not worthy of the love of Fernanda.

The first clue of the new day's dawn that appeared before Andreu's blurry vision was the familiar figure of Dona Catita who was busy getting ready to lift the shutters of her newspaper kiosk.

"Hello Andréu." Dona Catita said "What are you doing up so early? Are you getting some exercise so that you can return to playing baseball? Since you left, the team just keeps losing every match, so we could use some of your help, boy."

Out of politeness Andreu managed a false smile.

"But what's the matter with you Andreu?" Enquired Catalina when she observed his puffy swollen eyes.

"Come. Let's go inside. I'll make you a cup of coffee so that we have the perfect excuse for you to tell me what has happened." Like an automaton Andreu obeyed her, knowing that Dona Catita's concern was legitimate and that just possibly she could reveal to him the answers that he was looking for.

The noble woman was already well aware of Andreu's absence from home thanks to the mouths of his sisters, and with great tenderness she draped him with a blanket before handing him a cup of steaming coffee.

"Tell me my son. Tell me what is going on in that head of yours. Do you think it is fair that you have worried your whole family so much, with them not knowing where you were?" Andreu just fished his mother's letters out of his dirty pocket. By the look on her face Catalina clearly recognized those letters (and the story that they told from 25 years ago) and now fully understood the suffering that Andreu must have been going through. "I see your mother has finally decided to present you with the true story of who you are." After her usual pause followed by a forceful cough, Dona Catita continued. "A long time ago I advised her to show you these letters to alleviate your pain, but she always told me that she hoped she would never have to show them to you. So I guess something serious must have happened for you now to have them in your hands."

Andreu deduced that Catita knew more than she had ever let on and that he would not leave the kiosk without getting an answer to all of his questions.

"Tell me Catita. You knew about the existence of these letters, right? I know because you just recognized them instantly without me even needing to open them. Please I need to know what happened to my mother after John abandoned her."

"After your mother left John at the casino," she replied, "they never saw each other again. Months passed by and your grandparents were very hard on her, especially your grandfather who never, even on his deathbed, forgave her for having dishonored the family name. Worse was to come. Your grandfather still hated John so much that after the passing of nine months when you were born he just saw John reflected in you even though you were only a tiny baby. That really broke your mother's heart and in an act of total strength she ran away from the family home and came to shelter in my place. Of course I took her in with open arms and I also took care of you as if you were my own grandchild. For three years my home was your home and your mother's home until the day your grandfather died. "

"Your grandmother never forgave you for her husband's death, since she has always maintained that he died of sadness because of you. But with his death came a little calm, because your grandmother decided to forgive Socorro and invited her to return home. After time your mother decided to marry Gerardo Montiel, a drunken man, who had asked her to marry him and promised to take care of both of you. I was always strongly against this union, and unfortunately my intuition was right, because he always treated her so badly. But your mother never complained until that day when you intervened and dared to put a hand on him. That was enough to give your mother the courage to leave him. Years later I learned that your stepfather had known from the very beginning about the bet between John and the Russian and didn't say anything to your mother, since he saw the possibility there to get her for himself. He knew no one else would marry your mother after the scandal. Apparently, my Federico, rest his soul in peace, was also aware of this story, since he acted as a translator for John and his friend during their stay in Cuba."

As Catita confessed about the past Andreu could feel a thick knot forming in his throat. It was so thick that it prevented him from speaking, and yet at the same time his body revealed his deep suffering by trembling and the constant flow of tears down his cheeks. Andreu pressed the palms of his hands into his face. He finally understood how hard life had been for his poor mother.

"Why Catita? How did Mama Socorro endure so much rancor and hatred from everybody?"
"My child, only your mother can give you that answer, but whatever happens, I can only tell you that everything she has ever done was done for love."

Andreu didn't waste any more time. He left Dona Catita's and ran for home. He didn't stop running until he arrived there. The door opened, and as if by fate, it was his mother who had turned the door handle. His mother was the woman who had given him all of her love and care despite all the miseries, so he couldn't help himself; he just fell on his knees at her feet and broke down into the most sincere tears.

56
Love Between The Lines (third part)

While Andreu was weeping at his mother's feet, back in Spain, Carmen and Orlando had been in daily contact for two weeks, although not in person. They spoke on the phone, sent emails to each other and had even used Skype. And during that time, they got to know each other a little better. Carmen discovered that Orlando liked his own hands, not because he wrote great literature with them, but because he could feel things with them. "I am very happy with these appendages since they allow me to directly experience beauty." He had told her.

Orlando discovered that Carmen detested her own hands because she considered them ugly, blue and venous, sinewy and fibrous.

For two weeks, thanks to twenty first century technology, they studied each other and discovered many other things. He liked to examine the face of a woman, taking in her smile first and then her eyes; and then if he could see her body he would admire her breasts and then her hips and ass, always in that precise order. But Carmen scrutinized her men in other ways.

She liked to dive straight into their eyes, penetrate into their inky depths and finally imagine cerebral convolutions; she wanted to penetrate their thoughts. As for the body she agreed with Orlando and liked a good male ass, the kind that creates a shapely curve in the back of a pair of well-cut trousers.

When talking on Skype, Orlando looked at her lips and in his mind found himself licking them, but Carmen just stared into his hazel eyes, sensing his thoughts and spying on his soul.

Both resigned themselves to this new technology, remembering the old days, when without the help of a computer, young men and women would go out and physically meet each other, playing dominoes or cards in cafes, munching peanuts in a park or sniffing the personal and intimate perfumes of one another in High School corridors.

Their every day correspondence, on Skype, made them reveal their most personal secrets to each other. Carmen was not afraid of men, but they instilled in her some kind of respect, because in the past more than one of them had given her a good beating. In particular, she explained, there had been this powerful martial arts expert, a giant who had hit her in her floating ribs and left her breathless, and another one who had grabbed her by the hair and smashed her head against ground. Orlando The Great, on the other hand, did not seem to be scared of women ... "Well..." He specified. "I am very scared when they get angry." he went on to clarify "I don't like arguing with them, I don't like seeing them upset and since it takes two to fight, I prefer to simply turn the other cheek. "

What all the investigations and inquiries into each other's souls revealed was that, Orlando appeared to be dominated by his heart rather than his intellect by a ratio of 51 per cent heart to 49per cent intellect. On top of that Carmen discovered that he liked women to smell natural whereas she liked men to smell of perfumed woods, it was finally time for them to meet "in person".

57
True Love
(Seventh Letter)

Delicately and slowly, Socorro helped her son up from the floor where he was laying prostrated by his own lost pride. It was unusual to see him fallen, but at least his mother was there to encourage him to recapture his spirit.

"Mother, I have read your letters, and I'm thinking that I was the architect of the swamp in which you were immersed in silence throughout your entire life since you gave birth to me. You have tried to conceal the truth of my origin." Andreu whimpered as his eyes brimmed with tears. "How could you have carried such a heavy load all on your own?"

"My son, what load are you talking about?" Socorro replied as she stroked his hair, "You have not understood the purpose of these seven letters. Until today, I have been the prisoner of my own past, but now finally everything is over. My struggle with the past has ended and now it's your turn to divert the path of time and not repeat the same mistakes."

"I can't even fit the pieces of this puzzle together, mother." Andreu sobbed.

"Have you read all of my letters?" Mama Socorro asked.

"I didn't have the stomach to read the seventh, mother. Although I can deduce that only anger and tears could have been the ink of that last letter."

"Just give me the letter Andreu" Socorro asked her son and as she unfolded the paper, she continued.

"These final lines, my son, were not written for John. On the contrary they were written for a baby who was born in Bayamo's hospital 25 years ago, and who almost never met his own mother because I tried to take my life on more than one occasion before your birth. But fate would not permit me and instead gave me many years to pay a very high price for my mistake." Then she began to read out loud.

"My dear Andreu son of my heart:

Finally the day has come when for the first time your eyes have known the light and in which I have understood that there are more important and more infinite things in this life than the simple love of a man.

To feel your little body in my lap, warm and serene, has made me realize that you were not any currency to my equivocal acts. On the contrary, one day you will realize that you have become my engine, my strength and the inexhaustible source that makes me go on living.

You're my little Andreu and nothing and no one in this world will ever change that.

Your mom Socorro."

She dried her tears and folded the letter.

"It is now I who thanks you for your mere presence and your contagious warm and kind personality that seduces all around you". Mama Socorro continued. "You represent a role model for me, for your brothers and all your friends, but mostly I appreciate that you still have the ability to make me see the world differently. With you I feel the deepest love in the world: the mother's love. And this began just a few seconds after you were born.

As mother and son melted together into an embrace, Socorro returned that final letter to Andreu so that he could keep it, just in case someday he would need it. The rest of her memories simply vanished into the air, since her purpose had now been fulfilled.

"Don't allow Fernanda to become another Socorro, Andreu. She loves you more than any woman could ever love anybody in this world. The only difference between your story and mine is that unlike me she has found the perfect man who understands and complements her. If you leave her once again, I assure you that this time you will lose her forever, condemning her to make mistakes that she will regret for the rest of her life. Have you now resolved your doubts, Andreu?" She asked, to which Andreu nodded his assent. "You're not perfect my son, and will never be, but Fernanda thinks you are and I believe you would be making a serious mistake if you let her go."

Andreu finally understood the brutal truth. It was close on three weeks since he last heard anything about Fernanda. Could it be possible that the terrible confusion that he had caused on the day of their first intimate encounter since he arrived back in Cuba from New York had given Fernanda the wrong idea about his absence?

Andreu spent an entire hour reflecting and trying to retrieve, from beneath all the mental dirt that he had collected on the streets of Bayamo, the recalcitrant image that he possessed of Fernanda in his mind. He quickly regained his sanity. He placed a big kiss on his mother's cheek and like a bolt, he leapt from the porch of his family home, taking long steps to run through the streets of Bayamo to cross the void that separated him from Fernanda.

This was how Andreu went off to find the love of his life: his beloved Fernanda.

58
Love Between The Lines (final)

At the precise moment that Andreu was running to his Fernanda, Carmen Spain opened the door of her house. Her hair disheveled, her eyes bright and her mouth pink and half open. Orlando paused, paralyzed at the spot by the wild image he beheld before him. That lady was special. She seemed to have come straight from being chased by a satyr who had pursued her trying to sniff her like candy.

"May I come in?" Feeling slightly unsure of himself, Orlando asked politely, trying to be sure he didn't say anything that could possibly annoy the unpredictable Carmen.
"Why do you think I have opened the door for you?" She answered without any prior thought, she was of course just being herself, scathing to the bone.
"Sure." To Hell with my own thoughts - he thought to himself - she is the kind of woman that needs to be tamed...with love and care. Life has made her tough.

Orlando The Great stepped into the house and Carmen directed him towards the living room,
A dark place lined with books.

"Tell me then why you are here?" She demanded as she stood before him. Orlando remained silent for a long time while he took a gook look at her. He had discovered that this woman aside from having shapes and curves in all the right places also exuded a heady brew of sweet pheromones into the air.

"I have come on behalf of Mary Smith." He finally replied being careful to select exactly the right words.

Carmen sat down in an armchair and crossed her legs. She was dressed all in black. The black trousers with a black T-shirt belted at the waist emphasized her tiny waist. The T-shirt was also tantalizingly loose on her shoulders.

Sitting himself in the armchair opposite her, Orlando uttered the words "She's dead." Carmen drew herself forward arching her shoulders to look at him more closely.

The only thing between them was a small wooden table, upon which two empty cups, a sugar bowl, a milk jug and a pot of steaming hot coffee were standing.

"A promise is always a promise and I made a promise to her." He added after a long period of reflection.
"I agree." She replied as she filled the two cups with coffee. "Sugar?" she asked, Orlando nodded. "Milk?" Orlando nodded again and enjoyed a delicious moment, as Carmen's naked right shoulder presented itself to him. The gaping neckline of the black shirt had dropped capriciously to one side, leaving it exposed.
"She told me that you should keep on writing." Orlando eyes remained fixed on that shoulder. Carmen's well-defined clavicles reminded him of two beautiful protruding tree roots settled in the land of her skin.
"What For? What is the use of writing?" She whispered as she sipped her milk clouded, sugarless coffee.
"What's the use of breathing?" He replied as he sipped his.

At this point, Carmen realized that she had lost the battle because, in effect, what good is life for a writer without writing?

"Writing is a disease." Carmen said, just for the sake of saying something, as she finished her coffee.

"If it is a kind of illness, then why are you not in bed and having some rest?" Orlando sniggered and she infected by his levity laughed heartily.

"Are you Mexican?" She asked, changing the subject.

Orlando's eyes shone lively and expressive. A naughty smile crossed his face as he realized that she was now thawing towards him.

"Yes and are you Spanish?"

Right then Orlando was inspired to improvise, as the breasts of the Castilian lady were distracting him from his previously well thought out and planned topics of conversation.

"Does the violin really matter?" Orlando was shocked by his question.

"Which violin?" She asked as she poured each of them a second cup of coffee.

"What matters is the violinist, not the violin." He answered trying to make his point as calmly as he could. Carmen tilted her head to one side as she stated, "I can tell you are Mexican. You speak very strangely".

Orlando stopped to think for a moment, should he stop this game altogether, but he decided that he didn't want to lose for not trying, so he played on, once he had regained his mental balance.

"The purpose of my coming here is to convince you that you should continue writing." That was a lie as it was not the "sole" purpose of his visit.
"Orlando I don't want to and still I don't see the connection with violins." She replied as they both finished off their second dose of caffeine.
"Well." Orlando took a short pause to put his thoughts in order. "Have you ever read Italo Svevo?"
"Yes."
"And, isn't the violin like a mermaid? Only the heart of a hero can make a violin, or a mermaid, sing with the most sublime of sentiments." He shrugged as her eyes opened wide with the realization that what he had just said was true.
"Ah now I understand." She smiled sweetly as answered him. "What really matters is that both the violin and the violinist are needed to create the best work of arts."
"Yes." He added "You may have the most expensive violin in your hands, but if the violinist doesn't know

how best to caress its strings, the perfect violin will have no use."

"And what you want to do is to caress my strings, so that I start to write again?" She asked sarcastically.

Orlando hesitated before answering.

"No matter to me. I just came to see you here because I made a promise." And his face creased up into a frown.
"Okay. I'll think about it." She answered in a petulant tone. Orlando looked into her eyes trying to penetrate her thoughts. "Stop psychoanalyzing me. " She ordered him. "I really do not like anyone doing that to me."
"I'm not doing that." Orlando lied.
"Okay, I will start to write. Thank you for your recommendation and goodbye." She concluded getting up from her seat.

Orlando stood up too, but could not resign himself to leave the place just yet. She was already standing by the door and with her hand indicating the way out to him. Orlando left the living room as he was bid and walked down the hall towards the front door, where he paused to use his final strategy.

"Any chance of a kiss before saying goodbye." He asked somewhat coldly, but with a spark of mischief in his eyes.

"Why?" She replied in a sweet tone.

"So that you can find out how this violinist kisses." Orlando placed his right hand firmly on her waist and his left gently on her neck to draw her face towards his. Neither of them had time to use their reasoning or literary calculations, they kissed calmly, in the same way that a person drinks a glass of water, not out of thirst but out of pleasure. This was not a needy kiss the result of the fervor between two lovers. It was the sweet and mature kiss of two people who have already had thousands of painful experiences and knew very well about love and hate.

The touch of their lips brought comfort to each other, revealing to those tired minds, that they had already seen many things in their life and experienced many loves and hates.

A man and a woman may love each other not out of passion or romance, their youth, or the eroticism of the flesh. They may love each other simply with the tenderness of their two minds.

59
Where there was fire…

Tired and panting through lack of breath Andreu arrived at Fernanda's family home wishing to be reunited with his love.

Unfortunately for Andreu, Fernanda was not at home. Fernanda's habits had changed dramatically since Andreu hadn't turned up that night. From being a happy girl with a docile nature, now as each day passed, she insisted on displaying to the world that she was a cold-hearted woman.

Day after heartbreaking day Andreu religiously insisted on going to her home, and while on each occasion Fernanda refused to speak a word with him, Andreu didn't stop his daily visits. For hours he would wait there, motionless, in the hope that her heart would soften and she would forgive him.

It was only when the light of her room had gone out that Andreu would leave. Fearing that Fernanda had ceased to love him, he decided to do something forbidden. He secretly broke into her room to search for some indication of her feelings. Inside he discovered a drawer in her dressing table, where he found a written request made by Fernanda to Nestlé requesting to be transferred to a subsidiary elsewhere on the island.

He only had three days to convince her not to go.

Determined to win her back, Andreu left a letter under her pillow with the hope that she would read it before she left.

Dear Fernanda,

Over these last few days I have thought about you a lot, about how much I love and need you.
It is not surprising that you are the owner of each of my thoughts. Such is the importance to me of seeing you every day even from a distance that it mitigates much of my defeat.

I still carry in my mouth the taste of your lips, so sweet and warm. The idea of never seeing you again haunts me and I am afraid that the taste of you will only remain in my memories. I am very worried that your bedroom window will never open to illuminate my hope of seeing you again.

I know my recent behavior has put doubts in your heart. Please, you need to know it was my cowardice that was the reason that I didn't show up and clouded your thoughts, as you have never done anything wrong to me. That night when I didn't come to see you was not because of you, but because I thought I wasn't worthy of your love. I have hidden in the shadows of my thoughts over the past three weeks, thinking that I don't deserve you.

I am writing this note to you because I fear that I will never see you again. Only your tender glance can break the spell of my past mistakes. So I beg you not to leave. If you stay I promise that every day of your life you will live with no fear. Except the fear of knowing that every night I will want to rip your clothes off to possess you, to cover every inch of your skin with my kisses, the fear of sharing your breath.
Be only afraid that I would die for you.

Perhaps you still have your doubts about me. Believe me I do not blame you, but I cannot give up the hope that one day you will forgive me. I do not want to see you leave, because when you are gone I will be gone too. I will sit on the beach everyday to watch the sunset as a living memory of our love.

****

Two days passed. Andreu spent them on the beach watching the sun, his thoughts lost in the distance, as he looked inside his heart to find the strength to endure her departure.

As he stood there staring at the vast sea he detected a very familiar fragrance permeating the air. It was she, Fernanda, his Fernanda, whose mere presence was going to give him one last chance.

He took her by the waist and swept her off her feet, crushing her bosom into his chest in a tight embrace.

"You're back my love." Andreu sobbed. "I thought you wouldn't come because of what happened on that night, but please let me explain. I broke my promise to love you and worship us. I let myself get carried away by the love of the flesh, where I got hurt and I did a lot of damage. The day of my departure you confessed that you did not want to be the person who clipped my wings, but I know that if you go, my life will no longer have any meaning without you."

Fervently Fernanda took his hands and passionately kissed him.

"Reading the first line of your note was enough to tell me that there is still a vivid and pure love between us." Fernanda whispered into his ear. "I'm delighted to know that I can heal the wounds of your heart, and I feel that you have the strength to heal my broken wings. But what I want to know most is whether I am the love of your life."

"I just want this to be the beginning of our new story. I would die without the sound of your heartbeat. The rest ... Only time will tell and sentence our love." Andreu replied

And so as the two young lovers held each others hands they let their gaze get lost in the twilight, just as if their souls had agreed to a love pact for all eternity even before they met.

60
THE END

There is no love more valid than another because everyone loves the way he knows or can. There is no more affection in the romantic love just for the fact that one cradles or receives more caresses. Likewise the erotic love or even the pornographic love is not incorrect because they arise in perverse affection - but they are equally valid as long as they are consensual – as there are many humans who can not love in any other way because that is the only way they know.

The sound of a sweet love can be kind and affectionate, but the genuine cry of an orgasm can also become charitable and pious in an equal manner. Condemned by our innate or our acquired natures we love the way we know and the way we can. We are entitled to do so.

Experience teaches us to examine the eyes and words of those around us and discover whether they belong to the race of the romantic or the erotic. We can deduce that it is not a question of admitting or denying, but rather one of respecting.

Also our experiences instruct us in other kinds of glances -those with large eyes and weak and discolored faces belong to the frustrated ones in love or in sex. Bathed in sweat, those gigantic eyes criticize the love of others, but they themselves are repressed without actually deciding where to belong or love.

And to these latter we dedicate our final words; with which we hope they may regain some sanity.

Dare to love and feel with all your might, whether romantically, sexually or maternally as you please, but please love the way you know and the way you can, because while we are writing this, we must explain to you what is happening at this very moment now that you have arrived here with us.

At this precise instance, at the Miss MS Company the last wishes of Mary Smith are being fulfilled. Mr. Aldo Rocamora and Margaret have opened a window and with a sigh and a tear, have scattered Mary's ashes across the skies of New York.

Her vital force and that unbridled heartbeat are now only dust drifting through the air of The Big Apple. The human remains of her life are now being absorbed by the air and then simply spat out. Beware; maybe a mote of her ashes will fall on your head. You decide.

THE END

Made in the USA
Charleston, SC
23 September 2015